Prick*ly Promise (Prickly Proposal #2)

PRICK*LY PROMISE

The Prick*ly Proposal Series #2

Rachel Angel

1

Prick*ly Promise (Prickly Proposal #2)

Prick*ly Promise (Prickly Proposal #2)
Published by RomanceOnTheGoBooks.com; an Imprint of
Sparklesoup Inc.
Sparklesoup.com

Prick*ly Promise (Prickly Proposal #2)

Don't Miss a New Release from Kailin Gow! Sign Up for the Free Newsletter

sparklesoup.com

First Edition.
Printed in the United States of America.

AUTHORS' NOTE

Thank you for picking up Prick*ly Promise, the second book in the Prick*ly Proposal Duology Series.

This series is a New Adult Enemies to Lover Romance.

Prologue

<u>Priscilla</u>

It was one of those hot, dry days. The sun scorched the earth, and the dust floated into the air with every step I took. Looking out over the acreage Preston's ranch sat on, I was once again impressed with the magnitude of his success. The biggest sheep ranch in San Angelo... the biggest and most profitable sheep ranch in all of Texas... perhaps all of the country.

Despite the oppressive heat, I walked out past the barn in search of Preston.

Preston; my pretend fiancé, my bounty... my job. It was hard to believe that I'd become so attached to a man who could be so hard and cold, but I knew that my connection with him had become more than just an assignment.

Following the buzz of sheep shears, I walked around to the back – the shaded side – of one of the smaller storage buildings and found him.

Dripping with sweat, he sat on a short stool, holding a sheep between his legs with one hand while he shaved off the thick wool with the other. His tank top was drenched, and his dark blond hair curled at the nape of his neck.

I couldn't deny it. It was a pleasant sight and I just stood there watching him. With every move he made, his glistening biceps held me mesmerized. I chuckled to myself as the corner of my mouth rose in a crooked smile. Who would have ever thought that I would fall for a rancher?

The buzzing suddenly stopped, and all was silent.

"Hey," I said softly before he started up again.

He turned to me. His lips curved in a semblance of an appreciative smile as he looked me up and down, but his annoyance at my intrusion was clear in his dark eyes.

"What can I do you for?" he said as he wiped his brow with his forearm.

"Quite a day to be shearing, isn't it?" I said looking at the three other sheep nearby… waiting.

He slapped the back side of the sheep in front of him and the animal scooted away. "Just acquired them. It's downright abuse to leave these animals with this layer of wool on hot days like these."

I nodded. It was so easy to just talk about the weather, to discuss the well-being of the sheep and the other animals on the ranch. But at the back of my mind, there were so many more important things that I wished I could tell him.

Like the fact that his diabolical, biological father now knew where he lived, and it was all my fault. Preston Packard Prickly had made a life for himself far away from the clutches of his ruthless father and I, so proud to have found my bounty, had exposed him.

"Just wanted to see what you were up to," I lied.

With an arrogant shrug, he got up and went to the waiting sheep, got a hold of one and brought it back to his stool, then looked at me as he held up the shears. "This is what I'm up to."

Biting my bottom lip, I sought the best way to tell him. "Preston…"

"Yes?" he said as he glanced up at me, his shears ready to go.

How could I tell him that he now had to go into hiding? How could I tell him that the man that he loathed the most in the world was on his way over to see him?

And how could I tell him that it was all because I'd succeeded in doing my job… finding him?

"Priscilla?" he said, his finger on the switch of the shears he held aloft and ready.

I'd just spoken to my boss, Tip, who assured me that Mr. Jackson Prickly was determined to come to Preston's ranch.

"I… I was thinking about…"

"Spit it out now, Pris, or keep it 'til later."

"You know… um… I…"

The sudden buzz of the shears drowned me out as Preston turned his attention to the sheep between his legs.

Chapter 1

"I've changed my mind," I blurted out the moment Preston walked in the door. I'd been pacing back and forth in the kitchen, trying to calm myself by sipping on cold, tart lemonade.

"About what?" he said as he simultaneously pulled off his sweat-drenched tank top and kicked his boots off before heading to the bathroom.

"About Vegas," I said.

"I don't have time for that right now."

I followed him into the bathroom and watched him slip out of his jeans. What a beautiful man he was. I never tired of looking at him.

But now is not the time.

"Preston," I said, trying desperately to shake off the heated desire I had for him right there in that moment.

10

"Yeah?" He got into the shower and turned the water on.

"We need to get to Las Vegas," I said. "You promised that if I played along as your fiancé at that rodeo that you..."

"Yeah. Yeah. I know." He lathered up with a fragrant shower gel. "Fine. We can leave tomorrow. I'll let Bacon and Rick know."

"Not tomorrow, Pres. Today."

With his hair full of lather, he stopped mid-shampoo and looked at me. "Today?"

I nodded.

"Damn, Priscilla," he said as he resumed washing his hair. "I've been working since sunup dealing with those new sheep and I have a shipment of feed coming in this afternoon. It's a sixteen hour drive to Vegas."

"We can't drive. We have to fly. I've looked into chartering a flight. We could be in Vegas for dinner."

He rinsed off, shut off the water and opened the shower door. Stark naked and glistening with scented water, I literally let out a hungry sigh, causing him to grin that annoyingly knowing grin.

"What's the rush?" he said.

"We just have to be there today, okay?" I said.

"What… you got tickets to a show or something?" He shook the water out of his hair, patted himself dry with a fluffy yellow towel then wrapped the towel around his waist.

"Please, Preston," I said, not willing to get into an argument. "When you asked me to play your fiancé, I didn't give you a hard time and ask a bunch of questions… so could you please…?"

Heading into the bedroom, he looked at me with a crooked grin. "If I remember correctly, you did give me a hard time." He flicked off the towel and turned to his dresser drawer to pull out a fresh pair of boxer briefs.

"Please." I was right behind him.

"Fine," he relented. He turned to his closet and grabbed a pair of soft denim jeans. "Go get packed and we'll leave in an hour."

"I'm already packed and ready to go," I said as I pointed to my small overnight bag that was set on the decorative chair by the window.

Pressing his lips together, he pulled a red and blue striped button-down shirt off its hanger and shrugged it on as he glanced at the bag and back at me.

"I also packed you a few things," I added as I pointed to larger duffle bag on the floor by the door.

"So, I see." He stepped into a pair of dress boots.

"So?" I looked hopefully at him. "Can I arrange for that charter? I spoke with a Mr. Dickson, and he said he could be ready to take off in an hour and he's about twenty minutes from here."

"Yeah," he said with a grin. "I know where Dickson is. But I have a better idea."

"Better than a chartered flight that can have us in Vegas in a few hours? I don't think so."

"Grab that little bag of yours and follow me." He grabbed the larger duffle bag and headed out.

I was about to argue, but as he walked out of the room, I grabbed my bag and fell in step behind him.

Before exiting the house, he grabbed a cowboy hat off the rack and set it atop his damp hair. He opened the door and as we stepped out, Bacon and Rick came up the pathway.

"Where you off to, Boss?" Bacon said.

"The little lady wants a trip to Vegas," Preston said, gesturing to me with his chin. "I trust you guys will take care of the place?"

"Always do," Rick said.

"Have a good trip," Bacon added as we walked past them.

"Preston," I hissed as I came up beside him. He was heading to the barn. "What are you doing?"

"Going to Vegas," he said. "Isn't that what you want?"

I pointed to the barn that we were quickly approaching. "Yes... by plane, remember? What do you propose now? That we go by horseback?"

He chuckled. "I love how you underestimate me."

Frustrated, I rolled my eyes and sneered at the back of his head as he veered off toward the right.

So, it's not the barn?

Then where in the world are you taking me?

We walked past the sheep enclosure and beyond to the equipment building. I had no doubt that he had great big trucks and tractors and other machinery, but I couldn't for the life of me understand why he was leading me there.

I swear, Preston... if this is all a game to you, you're going to sorely regret it. I'm just trying to save you from the world of hurt that your dear old dad wants to throw on you... but, hey... if you want to play games...

Clamping my lips tight, I said not a word as he reached for the handle of the large sliding door and began to pull it back.

"Your chariot awaits, milady," he said with a flourish as the tall door slid back to reveal a small, single engine airplane.

My jaw fell. Like an idiot, I just stood there gaping at the plane. I suddenly understood the need for such an unusually large building, and I suddenly understood why there was a paved road that came out of the hangar and went nowhere.

Cat got your tongue?" Preston said with a smirk.

I finally shrugged off my indignation and entered the small hangar. "I thought you had a tractor in here."

"Nope," he said as he opened the passenger door to the plane. "This, my dear, is a Mooney M20 Acclaim Ultra. A single engine four-seater that will have us in Vegas in no time."

I nodded as I stepped closer.

"Made right here in Texas," he went on. "Well, that is, as of 2020."

I nodded again and I looked inside. It certainly was luxurious for such a small plane. The seats, covered in caramel and chocolate leather, beckoned me to reach out and touch the softness.

He had a plane. All this time he had a plane. He was just full of surprises.

"You know how to fly this thing?" I said, a little skeptical.

"We'll see." He cocked a playful brow as he held the door open for me.

"Hmm. Very funny." I looked at the interior of the plane and back at him.

"Well," he said. "Are you going to get in?"

"Seriously," I said, suddenly perplexed. "You know how to fly this thing?"

"Priscilla," he said in a slightly patronizing tone. "Do you really think that I would keep a plane on my property and invite you to fly to Vegas in that plane if I didn't know how the damned thing worked? Do you think that I would spend over half a million dollars just to keep this thing as a trinket?"

I shrugged. "I guess not." I climbed up and into the plane.

Chapter 2

Preston

From the corner of my eye, I saw Priscilla grip the hem of her long flowing blouse as we took off. Smiling, I considered doing a trick maneuver, but decided against it.

"You can breathe now," I said into the headset.

She didn't respond.

I nudged her and turned her headset on. "How you feeling?"

She shrugged.

"Are you afraid of flying?"

She shook her head.

"Well then, this should be a treat."

19

Keeping communication with the nearby control tower, I reached a respectable cruising altitude and then maintained a speed of nearly 200 miles per hour. As we came over the deserts of New Mexico, I once again communicated with control tower in the upcoming town and was cleared. The sky was mine. I was the only plane in the area.

With that settled, I decided to shake Priscilla up a bit. I let the plane dip down just enough to get her to grip anything she could get a hold of.

She glared at me. "You have a very distorted sense of humor, Mr. Packard."

I laughed then banked hard to the right, giving her a clear view of Roswell below.

"That's where the supposed UFO landed way back when," I informed her.

Unimpressed, she stared me down.

I reached out to hold her hand steady. "Sorry. I won't do it again."

She was silent for a long while, and then, "Are we going to make it to Vegas in one shot?"

"Nope," I said as I spotted a small and familiar airstrip up ahead. "We're going to be pulling into a small town just south of Albuquerque. I know a really great little taco place. Hungry?"

Staring straight ahead, she shook her head.

Moments later, I got the go ahead from the tower and made my approached and landed. "Smooth landing," I said.

The moment the plane was completely immobilized, Priscilla pulled off her headset and hopped out of the plane.

"Hey," I called out as I disembarked and went after her. "Where are you going?"

"I need some air," she shouted back.

I gestured to the attendant to gas up the plane as I ran to catch up with Priscilla. "How about those tacos I was telling you about?"

She stopped walking and turned back to face me. The corners of her mouth struggled to not smile as she tried to maintain an air of anger. She was amused but too angry to show me.

"Don't be mad at me," I said. "You're the one who wanted to fly to Vegas."

"And you're the one who is deliberately flying in a reckless fashion."

I grasped her shoulders. "And I apologized for that. I won't do it again. Now, do you want to grab a bite to eat or don't you?"

Biting down on a pleased smiled, she nodded.

I guided her out to the side street near the airstrip and found the small taco place on the corner.

"Wait out here," I said as I pointed to a small table out on the terrace. "I'll bring you out the best tacos you've ever had."

Her lips parted to argue, but I turned and headed inside and to the counter. "Two orders of fish taco," I said, holding up two fingers. "And two root beers."

Barely thirty seconds later, the two plates were set on a tray on the counter along with two tall glasses of root beer. I paid for the meal, grabbed the tray and headed out to Priscilla.

"You didn't ask what kind of taco I wanted," she said as I set a plate down in front of her.

"And what would you have asked for?"

"Fish taco."

"In a soft tortilla?"

"Yeah."

"Well, there you go."

With a skeptic grin, she pried apart her taco and looked inside. "Fish taco? How'd you know?"

"Intuition."

She took a bite and her eyes fluttered with pleasure. "Wow."

"Worth the flight?" I said.

She glared at me then smiled.

Eating our tacos took all of six minutes and we headed back to the airstrip. The plane had been refueled and was ready to go. We boarded the aircraft and put on our headsets.

"No smart tricks," Priscilla said as we took off.

I nodded and we took to the sky.

We passed over the black lava of El Malpais near Grants, then over the town of Gallup.. Priscilla looked down with interest as I pointed each of them out.

"I'd never noticed any of those," she said.

"How could you when you're flying at thirty thousand feet?" I said. "Now, wait until you see this."

Nearing Flagstaff, I veered off to the right and soon the vast chasm of the Grand Canyon came into view. With the sun low on the horizon, half the canyon was in the shadows while the other half was illuminated with golden light that made the canyon walls shine like copper and gold.

"Holy crap," she said. "I've been to the Grand Canyon a half dozen times and I've flown over it countless times, but I've never seen it like this."

I smiled, happy that I'd been able to show her something new. But as we approached Vegas, I paid closer attention to the air traffic around us.

Vegas. I'd never liked the city. It harbored far too many bad memories… thanks to my father. My heart suddenly pounded harder as I remembered the last time I'd visited the town.

I hadn't seen my father in years and when I'd graduated from high school, I thought I'd pay him a visit. In my naïve youth, I was hopeful… optimistic. Maybe he wasn't as bad as all the rumors I'd heard over the years.

Maybe Jackson Prickly did have a heart.

I arrived at the gleaming fifteen story Prickly Edifice which had luxury apartments on the top three floors and office space below. I parked my car just outside the entrance to the underground garage. It was late, later than I'd planned, but I was eager to meet with my father after all those years.

But as I stepped out of the car, I saw movement inside the dimly lit underground garage. I focused in and couldn't believe what my eyes were telling me. Shaking my head in disbelief, I focused in again and clearly saw two men hoisting a lifeless form into the trunk of a baby blue sedan.

I gasped, and as the men got into the car, I headed back to mine, got in and started the engine. I had no idea what I was doing or why, but I followed them. They left the city streets and went out to Lake Mead. As we entered the darkened park, I turned out my headlights and stayed far back. They pulled out onto a narrow dirt path that led to the lake's edge. I veered off into a rustic campsite, shut the engine and got out of my car.

Walking through the tall grass, I followed the red glow of their car's lights. The car came to a stop, the men got out and opened the trunk. The lifeless form now wiggled and struggled as the two men dragged him out of the trunk. His hands were tied behind his back causing him to lose his balance, fall to the side and bang his head on the car bumper. His muffled cries through the rag in his mouth mingled with the gentle lapping of the water and the rustling of the tall grass.

"You should have known better than to mess with him," one of the men said as he tied a cinder block to the man's ankle.

They dragged him to a rocky outcrop, banged him around a bit, then tossed the cinder block into the dark water. The man lurched a bit and one of the men gave him a final shove, sending him into the abyss.

I stood and stared for a moment, then turned to throw up. I felt sick. I was horrified. I was confused.

I was scared.

The two men got back in their car and drove off, leaving a cloud of dust as they passed me, hunched over in the tall grass.

As soon as they rounded the bend and were gone, I ran out to where they'd stood. On one side of the rocky outcrop that jutted out into the lake, the water was shallow, leading to a sandy shore, but on the other side the water was dark and deep.

I grabbed a dead branch and tried to poke around but found nothing. "Damn it," I hissed. I didn't know what to do.

Tossing the branch aside, I scrambled out of my sneakers, jeans and t-shirt and dove into the cool water. A part of me was creeped out by the thought, but a larger part of me knew that I had to find that person. He was still alive and if I could find him and drag him out, I could save him.

But it was futile. I was blind in the dark water and feeling my way around brought no results. After my third dive down, I got out. Whoever that man was, he was probably dead by now.

Shaken up, I grabbed my clothes and headed back to my car. Finding my phone on the passenger seat, I called the police.

"9-1-1. What's your emergency?"

"Uh…" Damn it. How could I tell her what I'd just seen. She wouldn't believe me. "I… I just saw a man fall into Lake Mead."

"Where exactly on Lake Mead did you see this?"

I gave her directions as best as I could, all while trying to better explain what I'd seen. By the time she hung up with me, a police car was coming up the path.

I ran out to meet them.

"You say a man fell into the water?" the first police officer said as she got out of the car.

"Yeah," I said as I led the way to the water's edge. "Right over here. I dove in and tried to find him, but…"

"We'll take it from here, son," the second officer said.

"He was…"

"You're shaken up," the first officer said. "That's understandable, but you can go home now. We'll take care of it."

I wanted to tell them more, tell them about the two other men, tell them how I'd followed them out here, but the police seemed uninterested.

I turned and headed back to my car, got dressed and slowly and numbly made my way to my casino hotel that was right on The Strip. In a daze, I checked in then boarded the elevator and found my room.

Inside, I barely noticed the outdated décor and the slight scent of moisture. I was just happy to be away from the world and alone with my thoughts.

Exhausted, I got undressed and took a long hot shower. Even after thoroughly washing and rinsing off, I could smell the remnants of the lake's water on me. It was in my nose, in my nostrils… in my head.

I sat on the edge of the bed and turned on the television. Perhaps the news channel would mention the missing person. But as I waited for the news story that never arrived, I grabbed the phone to make a call.

"At this hour, it better be good," the old grumpy voice said.

"Uncle Packard? It's Preston."

"Preston? Where the hell are you?"

He'd raised me when my mother couldn't afford to raise me after my jerk of a father left us.

A good old boy, he had a way with me that made me the man that I was. While he'd always allowed me plenty of freedom, he also kept a close eye on me and kept me out of trouble, kept me in line.

"I'm in Vegas," I said a little sheepishly.

"Vegas? What the hell for?"

"Don't be mad, Uncle Packard, but I came to see my father. I thought... after all this time. I mean... I'm a man now. I'm not just a child."

"Get your behind back home, Preston."

"What? Why? He's my father. I have a right to see him and get to know him."

"Preston. Your father is not a kind man. I don't know just how you've come to romanticize this man, but he is not what you imagine."

"I've heard rumors, Uncle Packard, but..."

"Believe those rumors, Preston. Believe them. Your father is ruthless. Oh, he might not get his hands dirty by doing anything himself, but he has hired hands who will do the deed for him. Whether it's breaking a leg as a warning, torturing a competitor for information or killing a man who's wronged him... his men will get the job done."

"But..." I thought of the two men carrying that man out of the trunk of their car.

"Get out of there before you father finds out that you're in town."

I had done as he'd told me and had gone back to San Angelo. Thinking of him now, I smiled. He'd been a man of few words, but the impact of those words would stay with me forever. A large part of me still mourned his death. He'd meant so much to me. He'd been so kind and generous.

"You okay?" Priscilla said as she looked at me with concern.

I glanced at her. The pretty blond girl with a smile that could light up a room, with a body that could make any man swoon and with a head that made her a successful bounty hunter. She had it all, and she'd come all the way out to San Angelo to find me… for Jackson Prickly.

Shit. What was I about to let myself get dragged into? And why?

Soon the airport came into view.

"Sin City, here we come," I said, ignoring her question.

Shaking off my nostalgic foray, I made my approach, received my clearing to land, and then taxied to a stop.

"Smooth as silk," I said as we got out and grabbed our bags. "Where to?"

She looked at me with a tired grin. "Right now, all I want is to find a hotel room, take a good long shower and fall into a warm, soft bed.

"What… no casino? No show? No night on the town?"

She laughed. "Not for me. Not tonight."

We got into a hired car and were soon getting out at one of the finest hotel's Vegas had to offer. After checking in, we headed up to the seventeenth floor to our room.

"Feels just like home," she said as she set her bag down on the dresser and headed to the window. "Just look at all that sin walking around down there, looking for a good time, looking to strike it rich, looking to be mesmerized by a spectacular show. Isn't this the greatest town on earth?"

I laughed as I kicked off my boots. "I happen to think that San Angelo is the greatest town on earth, but hey... I am kind of partial."

She smiled that playful smile as she passed me by and headed into the bathroom. Just before closing the bathroom door, she tossed out her shirt and bra.

Was that an invitation? Well, I sure hope so.

I heard the gush of water then the gentle sound of her voice as she sang an old show tune. Peering inside, I saw her, exquisite in her glistening nudity as she tilted her head back to let the warm water run down her long hair.

Without saying a word, I undressed and stepped into the shower stall with her.

"Hey," she said when she opened her eyes and saw me. "You took a shower back home before leaving."

"You can never be too clean," I argued. "Besides, you seem awfully dirty. I thought I'd come in and help get you washed up."

"Dirty?" she said with surprise. "I'm not dirty."

"Oh, yes you are," I said, my voice suddenly dropping to a sultry tone. Grasping her shoulders, I turned her around, grabbed her hands and leaned over her to press her hands to the shower wall.

"What are you doing?" she said through a playful laugh.

I squirted some shower gel into a washcloth and proceeded to wash her back with long gentle strokes. I then moved down to wash the length of her shapely legs and onward to her feet. Having kept the best for last, I ventured up to carefully wash her ass. I scrubbed her cheeks, parted them and ran my fingers between them.

Groaning, my desire for her, I turned her around and washed her arms and her belly and finally, her breasts that beckoned me with their pert nipples.

"You forgot my face," Priscilla said.

I reluctantly left her breasts and gently scrubbed her face.

"And my hair," she added as I prepared to return to her breasts.

I dutifully washed her hair and rinsed the suds out.

"Now?" I said, holding my hands aloft over her breasts.

"Now," she said with a nod.

I nuzzled between the two generous mounds, kissing one then the other as my hand slid down between her legs.

36

She let out a soft groan, then a sigh and then a quiet squeal as I worked her up. "Fuck me," she whispered into my ear.

I leaned her up against the shower wall and my cock easily glided inside her. My entire body responded to her, felt her, wanted more of her, and as I climaxed, I knew that I would want her again soon.

"I guess I wasn't as tired as I thought," she said as she raked her fingers through my hair.

Resting my arms on the wall on either side of her head, I leaned in to kiss her. "I think that asking you to pretend to be my fiancé for the rodeo was the best thing I ever did."

"Is it, now…" she purred.

"And if paying you back for that favor means coming out here, well… I'm happy to do it. I'm a man of my word."

"And I'm happy to hear it."

I was still apprehensive about the prospect of meeting with my father, even if that was the ultimate task that she'd been hired for.

Brushing wet strands of hair off her brow, I looked into her eyes and wondered if she knew just how ruthless and cruel my father could be. Did she have any idea what she'd gotten herself into?

Either way, I was going to do everything within my power to ensure her safety. I was prepared to do anything to protect her... anything.

"I love you," I whispered through the spray of warm water.

Chapter 3

Priscilla

"Are you ready to hit the Strip?" I said as I stepped out of the bathroom dressed for a night on the town.

While I had loved my time in San Angelo, I was eager to get reacquainted with my town. After a long and lazy morning in bed, I was also looking forward to showing Preston around.

"Whoo-wee! Look at you."

As Preston had nodded off the night before, I'd taken a few minutes to do a little online shopping and had found a gorgeous shimmering silver mini dress with crystal encrusted spaghetti straps that

39

crisscrossed down my otherwise bare back. It was sexy, cute and fun.

I shimmied and shook my backside at him. "Be ready to see Vegas like you've never seen it before," I promised him.

"And all I have is a pair of jeans."

I walked up to him and squeezed his cheeks together, effectively squishing up his lips. "Don't worry, baby. I've got you covered."

I turned to the closet and pulled out the latest designer blood red dress shirt.

He tugged off his white t-shirt and shrugged on the dress shirt.

"You're set and ready to go," I said, slipping my feet into the elegant silver sandals I'd ordered along with the dress.

We headed out and took the elevator down to where all the action was. Already, the lobby was abuzz with check-outs and new arrivals. We walked out and merged into the crowd that had already taken up the sidewalks of the Strip. We stopped here and there to take a look, window shop and even went into a few of the souvenir shops.

It was a gorgeous day that was already heavy with the late afternoon heat, but it didn't stop people from going out to enjoy the day.

Strolling down the Strip, I suddenly grabbed Preston's hand and pulled him into a casino.

"Come on," I said. "Let's try our luck at the slots."

"I'm more of a poker man, myself," Preston argued as he followed me inside.

We got twenty dollars' worth of change and meandered up and down the aisles looking for the perfect opportunity.

"Over there," I said, pointing to an old man as he slid off his stool. "Look at him. I'll bet you anything that he's been sitting at that machine for hours."

"Yeah, he does kind of look worn out."

"That's the machine that we need." I grabbed the sleeve of Preston's shirt and tugged him along as I marched toward the departing man.

"Huh?" Preston said as he looked down at me. "Why that one?"

"He's been throwing money into that slot machine, and it hasn't paid up."

"How do you know?"

I pointed to the top of the machine. "That thing is ready to pay out two thousand, three hundred and thirty seven dollars."

Impressed, Preston looked at me then back up at the top of the machine. "But what makes you think it's ready to pay out?"

From the corner of my eye, I caught sight of an elderly woman, her big plastic coin-filled cup in hand as she headed toward the newly vacated slot machine. I quickened my step reaching the stool miles ahead of the old woman.

"I think that woman wanted that machine," Preston said, forever the gentleman.

"I know," I said adamantly. "That's why I rushed the stool."

"There's a perfectly good slot machine right there." He pointed to a vacant machine at the end of the aisle.

I glanced up at him. "Amateur."

With a fistful of coins ready, I half sat on the stool and fed that machine. "This thing is just bursting at the seams and ready to make somebody rich."

He chuckled as he leaned up against the machine and faced me. "You sure are concentrated on that thing."

"I take playing the slots very seriously," I said, glancing up at him with a playful grin.

With barely six dollars played, the bells and whistles announced to everyone around me that I'd won. Preston looked at me in amazement.

"Oh, my God. I can't believe it. You won."

"Told you she was ready to burst."

The elderly woman who'd wanted my machine glared at me as I let out an excited squeal and left the machine. I handed her the remains of my twenty dollars in change and wished her good luck.

"Dinner's on me," I said as we walked out of the casino with my winnings tucked away in my purse.

I led the way to an elegant and fancy seafood restaurant, and we were swiftly seated at an intimate table.

We ordered a nice bottle of wine and a shrimp appetizer.

Just as I prepared to take my first bite, my phone rang. Shooting an apologetic glance at Preston, I pulled out my phone and took a look.

Priscilla, where are you?

"Damn it, Tip," I mumbled as I bit my lip. What awful timing.

I'm right here in Vegas, Tip… just like you told me. I have my bounty right here in front of me.

I stared at the screen as I awaited his response.

Not sure that's a good idea. I'll get back to you in a bit, he wrote back.

Frowning, I tried to understand the cryptic message.

"What's up?" Preston said.

"Not sure yet." I put my phone away and tried to enjoy the remainder of our dinner.

But I couldn't shake Tip's message. Why was it not a good idea to be in Vegas. That was what I'd been tasked to do.

After licking my dessert plate clean and finishing my coffee, I looked at Preston who'd foregone a dessert.

"The water show at the Bellagio should begin in five minutes. I'd hate to miss it," I said as I took care of the tab.

"Water show?"

"Yeah. Come on."

With only the faintest remnants of sunlight detectable, we walked out onto the Strip and made our way through the crowds arriving at the Bellagio just in time.

The moment the sprays of water began to spout up in their fluid dance, Preston let out a surprised gasp.

"I can't believe you've never seen this before," I said with a pleased smile. I was happy to have introduced him to something so spectacular. "Haven't you ever seen Ocean's Eleven? It was featured in that."

He shrugged.

My phone rang before the end of the show. Tip. Damn it. I backed away from Preston to take the call.

"Tip, what's going on?"

"I'm on the Strip. Where the hell are you?"

"The Bellagio. Tip, will you please tell me what's going on?"

"Jackson and his men are still in town."

Damn. "Are you sure?"

I turned around and, in the distance, through the crowd of onlookers, I saw him. He'd spotted me as well. Despite his age, he was coming toward me with a determined step.

"Priscilla, man am I glad I found you," he said as he wiped his sweaty brow with the palm of his hand.

Preston came up behind me and put a possessive arm around my shoulder.

Tip glanced up at Preston then quickly scanned the crowd to our right and then turned to scan our left. It wasn't like him. He was usually such a calm man, always in control. But now he was clearly on edge.

He turned to me suddenly, his eyes hard... all business. I knew that look in his eyes. I'd seen it before. Years earlier, after my father had gone to prison, Tip had come to my family home and had confiscated all of our belongings.

It had been my introduction to the world of bounty hunting.

But now, seeing him here, so agitated... it was disconcerting. I had called him earlier to let him know I wasn't bringing my bounty to Jackson Prickly. I wasn't following through with the bargain. Then I had let Jackson Prickly himself know he wasn't going to get his son delivered to him like he thought. Now that I had reneged on my deal, I had gone rogue. Seeing Tip in person was not good.

"Babe, this is my boss and mentor, Tip," I said. I turned to Tip. "This is my date."

"Nice to meet you," Tip said. He looked at me and winked. "It's about time you went out on the dating scene."

He had that paternal gleam in his eyes, but I couldn't help but look past it and wonder why he would tell me that Jackson Prickly was around.

"I'm enjoying this night on the town, Tip," I said, trying to impart on him how I wanted to continue to enjoy my evening. "You shouldn't be here," I added, leaning closer to him.

"I had to find you," he said softly.

"You and me... if we're seen together... This isn't good, Tip. If people discover that we work together..."

"I won't stay long." He looked around. "I just wanted to be clear."

I wanted to ask how he'd tracked me down. It was normal for him to text me or call me... but to actually show up in the vicinity of my presence. A chill ran up to the nape of my neck. Something was up.

Our eyes met and I felt a tension that I'd never felt between us before.

He was all business. Bounty hunter and nothing personal.

I thought he would understand what I did. Didn't bring in my bounty at first. For Preston's sake. But then...

Tip was the one who called me to tell me Jackson Prickly was headed to San Angelo to get Preston himself. Tip had seemed like he was warning me. Get out of San Angelo now, and bring Preston with you.

Turns out, Tip had tricked me. Lied to me. To get me to bring Preston to Las Vegas after all. Where Tip would be delivering Preston to his father himself. Take me out of the whole transaction, and collect the bounty himself.

Then, as I looked at the hard line of his lips, it dawned on me. He didn't just want me out of the Prickly case, but he wanted me completely out. The look in his eyes, cold and oddly veiled.

He wanted me dead. He wanted me out of the way... and how many other bounty hunters wanted me out of the way as well? How many of Jackson's men, his goons, his henchmen, his assassins wanted me gone?

I'd fallen into the trap and had made myself a target. I should have known he was not to be trusted.

50

When he destroyed my life by confiscating everything under my father's name, he had been working for Jackson Prickly, the man who accused my father for some kind of crime against Prickly. Tip had always been a bought man for Jackson Prickly.

Never trust someone who can be bought.

Tip had told me this early on when he was teaching me how to be a bounty hunter. How right he was.

"You chose the wrong side, Pris," Tip said, shaking his head. "All you had to do was finish your job." A small shake of his head was the only indication that he ever felt like a father-figure to me. "You brought this on yourself. Action has consequences."

I knew what he meant now. I was out. No longer a bounty hunter. No longer privy to any of the secrets I held about Tip and the guys he worked for. I was out. Out. As in there was only one way out for someone who has gone "rogue". And now

Prick*ly Promise (Prickly Proposal #2)

Vegas was the most dangerous place on earth for me… and for Preston.

Chapter 4

<u>Preston</u>

I caught the concerned look in Priscilla's eyes and the cold response from her bounty hunter handler.

Tip; he initially appeared to be an easy-going and affable character, but that had quickly faded, and his eyes were now as hard as ice cubes.

He looked at me with suspicion and I had little doubt that he hadn't fallen for Priscilla's 'date' introduction. No. He knew who I was, and he clearly didn't like it.

Priscilla had brought me to Las Vegas, but she had neglected to go through with actually delivering me to the man who'd set her up on this chase.

Why?

I looked at her and tried to understand what was going on.

We'd arrived in Vegas the night before and I'd expected her to push for a meeting with my father.

But she hadn't.

I'd shrugged it off. We were both exhausted and wanted a good night's sleep.

This morning, I'd once again expected her to bring up my father, but when she suggested a relaxing morning then heading out on the town, I'd thought... why not? I'd been to Vegas before but had never done the tourist thing.

But now... Now as I looked at her, it became more and more clear that she was deliberately delaying my meeting with my father.

Why?

I shifted my gaze to Tip who seemed eager to follow through for her. He teetered back on forth, from the heel of his feet to his toes. He seemed ready to pounce on me at any moment.

Without warning, Priscilla grabbed my arm and quickly ushered me away from Tip.

"What's going on?" I muttered, looking back at the man who was supposedly Priscilla's boss.

"Come on."

I glanced back once again, this time spotting the two behemoths behind Tip. I'd seen those behemoths before... my last trip to Vegas.

As I turned to look ahead of me and follow Priscilla through the crowd, I tried to tell myself that it was just an illusion. It was just my horrible memories coming back to haunt me.

But I knew that wasn't the case.

I shot a look back again and saw them. It was them. There was no mistaking it. As much as I had tried to forget them over the years, their ugly mugs were etched into my memory.

If they were there, how far could my father be? Was Jackson Prickly just around the corner, waiting?

What sort of welcome are you planning for me, Daddy? I thought with a sneer.

If his henchmen were on the look-out for me, I seriously doubted he would greet me with open arms.

With a burst of adrenaline pumping through my veins, I grabbed a hold of Priscilla's hand, took the lead and plowed through the crowd.

The Bellagio was far behind us, but head and shoulders above the crowd, the henchmen came after us with Tip struggling to keep up.

Shit, I thought as they got closer. I tried to push Priscilla to run faster.

"These sandals are for dinner and dancing, not sprinting down the Strip," she said as she did her best to keep up.

"Hang on," I said as I swiftly picked her up and threw her over my shoulder. "Hang on!"

I ran as fast as I could, but the crowd of surprised and amused tourists hindered me.

"Out of the way!" I shouted with a broad and eager grin on my face. "Newlyweds here. Newly married. Out of the way. We're heading to our honeymoon suite."

That was enough to clear the way. People smiled, applauded, wished us well and one elderly couple even threw a handful of confetti at us as we passed them by.

"Back there is her disgruntled father and abusive brothers!" I shouted. "They want to stop us."

The crowd, eager to see us get our married life off on the right foot, tightly closed ranks behind us, doing a surprisingly good job at slowing Tip and the henchmen down.

Breathless and sweating, I ran into our hotel lobby. Not wanting to wait for an elevator, I turned into the stairwell and finally slowed down.

"You can let me down now," Priscilla said.

Smiling, I glanced at her partially bare ass that was right there by my cheek. "Nah," I said with a smirk. "I'll carry you up to our room."

"I think Tip might know where we're staying," she said, unamused. "We need to get our things and get out."

Sobering up quickly, I set her down and looked at her. "What the hell is going on? Really going on…"

"Let's go up to our room, grab our things and get out of here," was all she said.

Chapter 5

<u>Priscilla</u>

What could I tell him? That his father was after us? That my boss and mentor might have turned on me? I barely knew myself how everything had turned sour so fast. The last hour had completely turned my world upside down and I still hadn't figured out how or why.

As soon as Preston set me down, we walked up to the third floor, checked the hall, then went out to the elevator. We kept our distance as the doors slid open and, once certain that none of our pursuers where there, we got in and took the elevator the rest of the way up.

We reached our room, I pulled out the cardkey and tried to open the door.

Increasingly frantic, I jiggled the doorknob. "Shit," I let out. "Come on. Now's not the time to fuck with me. Why the hell won't you open?"

"Here," Preston said, keeping his calm. He took the cardkey from me. "Let me try."

On his first attempt, the door immediately unlocked, and we rushed in.

I quickly kicked off my shiny little sandals and slipped into my tennis shoes.

"Smart move," Preston said.

With a nod, I shoved everything I had into my small bag, including my new sandals, while Preston grabbed his duffle bag.

"Ready?" I said, my bag over my shoulder.

"For what?" he said, clearly angry with the turn of events. "What's waiting for us outside that door, Pris? Outside this hotel? My father practically owns half this town. How do you propose we stay out of his grasp?"

"By staying one step ahead of him," I said as I headed for the door.

He didn't move.

"Preston. Are you going to trust me or are you going to take a chance that your dear old dad just wants a nice little chat with his long-lost son?"

With his lips tightly pressed together, the corner of his mouth rose with contempt. "Okay. Go on," he said as he came to me and gestured for me to lead the way.

I opened the door and checked the hallway. "All clear," I whispered to Preston.

With Preston right behind me, I rushed out of the room and ran down the carpeted hallway, leading Preston to the staircase at the back end of the hotel. With surprising speed, we ran and jumped our way all the way down to the basement level and then out the back door.

"This way," I whispered.

Preston hesitated.

"Trust me."

"That seems to be the theme of this trip."

"Well… do you have a better idea?"

He shook his head and followed me down a narrow street, then we turned left.

"Do you know where you're going?" he whispered. "It looks like you're leading me to a junkyard."

"Not quite," I said. I shimmied through an opening in the chain link fence that surrounded a small car repair shop.

"What the hell? Are you going to steal a car?"

I chuckled as I walked up to the door of the shop, pulled a key out from behind the spare tire that was leaning up against the wall and opened the door.

"Come on. Hurry," I said, shoving Preston inside.

Once inside, I headed to a plain gray, non-descript sedan. I reached under the passenger door and retrieved a small magnetic key holder.

"Seriously?" Preston said.

"Just a little thing I keep in case of emergencies," I said, unlocking the door.

"Couldn't you find something more... recent. This is the dullest looking car I've ever seen."

"That's the point," I said as I patted the hood of the car. "This is my 'shit hits the fan' car. It's not meant to catch anyone's eye. It's meant to just melt into the flow of traffic. Just another plain looking grey sedan... a ghost."

"Does your mentor boss know about this place, and this car?" he said as he looked at the vehicle with open disgust.

I smiled my most devious smile. "Hell, no." I turned to the vending machine. "Want something to drink?"

"A beer would sure be good."

"Coming right up." I headed into the small office where a mini fridge was kept under the desk. I pulled out two beers and headed back to Preston who'd helped himself to a seat in my 'shitty' car.

"Here you go," I said as I got into the driver seat and handed him his beer.

He opened his beer and downed half its content in just a few gulps.

"Not so fast," I said as I took a small sip of mine. "I want to calm you down, not wipe you out."

He chuckled. "It's going to take a whole hell of a lot more of this stuff to wipe me out, especially now." He turned to face me. "Now... What's going on?"

I took in a deep breath. "While we were in San Angelo, I got a tip that your father was on his way there to find you. I don't know if he was losing patience or simply losing faith in my abilities. Either way... I realized that you were in danger, so... Well, I thought I would just get you out of there... far from danger."

"And now?"

"Well, now... it appears that the danger is right here... in Vegas."

"How?"

"What do you mean, 'how'?"

"How can my father know that I'm here in Vegas and not still in San Angelo?"

"I don't know. I haven't figured that out yet."

"What about your boss?"

"Tip?"

"Yeah. You think he might have snitched and told my father where to find me?"

"I don't see why he would. I mean…" My voice trailed off as I tried to make sense of it all. I'd known Tip for a long time, but… did I really know him?

"I wouldn't put it past my father to pay your boss off and get him to do whatever the hell he wants him to do. That's his way. That's who he is. No matter what, things have to go his way."

He looked at me, his eyes softening with concern. "I wouldn't be surprised if he wanted you taken out, as well. You've become a liability. In his eyes, you've betrayed him, and that's a crime punishable by death."

I nodded, then shook my head. While I'd been a little apprehensive about Tip myself, I couldn't imagine that he would really sell me out. "Your father might want me out of the way, but I don't think he went through Tip. Tip is a bounty hunter through and through, even if it is personal. He has his reputation to think about. If word got out that he was bought out... No. He wouldn't do that."

Preston looked at me, his brow high and full of doubt.

"No," I repeated. "He doesn't think of anything as personal." DON'T UNDERSTAND THESE LINES.

"He wasn't alone, you know," Preston said.

"What do you mean?"

"Tip. Your boss. I saw my father's men behind him when we were leaving that water fountain show."

I frowned. His father's men? "How do you know? What do you know about your father's men?"

He waved my question away. "It's a long story. Suffice it to say that I've seen them before, and I've seen what they're capable of. These aren't the type of guys you want to get mixed up with."

"I've seen plenty of the Vegas underworld. I know about the rats that live down there."

"Really? And do these rats kill inconvenient men and toss them into Lake Mead with a cinder block as a token anklet?"

I looked at him, wondering what he really knew about these men. Had he really seen them throw someone into the lake or was it just his imagination going wild?

"Look," I said. "Tip gave me this assignment... to find you and tell you about your inheritance."

Preston scoffed. "Like I need that bastard's fucking dirty money."

"I was to bring you back here to meet with your father. That's all I know." I looked at him wondering how everything had gotten so mixed up.

"This was actually supposed to be a very simple assignment. That day at your ranch… all I had to do was show you that envelope, show you what was coming to you and fly you back to Vegas." I clapped my hands together in a 'job done' manner. "It wasn't supposed to be so complicate, certainly not to the point where we're now hiding in here."

"Yep," Preston said. "That man is full of surprises."

"Who is he, Preston?" I said. "I mean, what does he really want with you? A father doesn't go chasing after his son just to pass on his wealth. There has to be more to it than just that."

Preston shrugged and sank back into the car seat. "Dear old dad. My biological father. I didn't even know he was alive for all of my childhood. The bastard just up and ran out of our lives – my mom and me – and I didn't even know what he looked like. Then, out of nowhere, he came back into my life… the type of man you'd never want to know, and I learned that fast enough."

He turned to look at me, his eyes red with unshed tears. "I know that this is going to sound crazy, but I think he killed my mom. I really do."

I stared at him in disbelief.

"And now, I think he wants to kill me. Why?" He shrugged. "I have no fucking idea."

"The man is just evil," I whispered.

"You can say that again."

I felt numb. I felt faint.

"I should have never taken this assignment."

He nodded in agreement.

"What could your father want with me?" I said. "When I backed out of bringing you to him, he threatened me with something about my father. Why? What's the connection?"

"I wish I could tell you. I wish I could tell you what that man has in his head. I've done all I can to stay away from him these past years. If you remember how I greeted you when you arrived at my ranch... when I saw my father's name on that manilla envelope..."

I laughed. "Oh, yes. I remember that."

"Well, that ought to tell you how little I appreciate the man."

I set my nearly untouched beer aside and got out of the car to go through my little travel bag.

"What are you looking for?"

"Less conspicuous clothing. I'm as visible as a disco ball in this thing."

"Yeah. One hell of a sexy disco ball."

I chuckled as I found a pair of cutoff jeans and a plain gray t-shirt.

As I shimmied out of my silver dress, I caught Preston's gaze and smiled, then quickly threw on my shorts and shirt.

"Do you think they'll find us here?" Preston said, his gaze still fixed on my breasts even though they were now covered with the thin fabric of my faded t-shirt.

"No, but I want to be ready if they do." I got back into the car and turned to face him. "I have something to tell you."

"Sure. Shoot."

"Years ago, my father ran a security company. It was very successful and well established. He was good at what he did."

"So that's where you get the brains from," he said with a grin.

"When I was in college, I found out that my father had been accused of a crime and had been sent to prison."

"What'd he do?"

"I'm absolutely sure that he never did anything wrong… nothing illegal. But what was he accused of? I have no idea. Fraud? Embezzlement? Laundering? Whatever the case, I know that my father would never do anything like that."

"What happened after that?"

"Tip showed up."

Preston looked at me with a confused frown. "To come help out the family?"

I let out a quick laugh. "Oh, no. No. No. No. He came to take away what little we had left. Furniture, computer, car, all of it."

"I don't get it," Preston said. "This guy came into your life, took everything from you and now you work with him?"

I shrugged. "What can I tell you? I had nowhere to go. And, you know what… there was something about what he did for a living… something exciting and adventurous and… Well, I really pestered him to hire me. At first he wanted nothing to do with me. I mean, I was just a kid in his eyes. He even suggested that I become a model or something like that. Imagine that."

"I can certainly see that happening," he said with a grin.

I glanced up at the ceiling of the car. "Anyway, I persisted, and I even convinced him and … voila. I became one of the most successful bounty hunters in the area."

"So, Tip worked for my father back then," Preston said.

"So did Tip worked for my father back then?" Preston said.

I looked at him. "I never thought about it, but it just hit me that he did. You're right. Tip works for Prickly. He's probably always worked for him."

Preston nodded.

"And that's why he was the one to come and take away all of my family's belongings."

He nodded again.

I slammed my palms against the steering wheel. "Damn. Why didn't I see it years ago? How could I have missed it?"

"I'm guessing that your boss and mentor is really good at hiding things." He reached out to put his hand over mine. "Besides, you were probably too deeply imbedded in your personal pain to really see clearly. You had nowhere to turn, and he took up the paternal role in your life. The way you tell your story, you didn't even have friends or relatives to take you in." He shook his head as he reflected. "I guess I was lucky that I had my uncle at the Packard Ranch to take me in when things everything went bonkers. I can't imagine being left on my own."

"Yeah," I muttered, suddenly feeling all alone again, just like I had back then.

He squeezed my hand.

"I'm sorry," I said. "If I'd known about any of this. If... Damn. I was effectively hired to find you and lead you to your father like a sacrificial lamb. I... I just can't..."

"Don't be so hard on yourself," he said with another squeeze of my hand. "You didn't know. You couldn't have known."

I shook my head. "No. I should have known. I should have looked into it. I should have found out who I was really dealing with."

He reached over to cup my cheek and leaned in to kiss me. Surprised, I backed away before finally giving in to the kiss. His lips were tender

74

and forgiving. When he pulled away, I looked into his eyes in amazement.

"You're not angry with me?" I said.

He shook his head. "Of course not. I know that you're not responsible for any of this. He is."

"I've disrupted your life and now I've led you into danger... the last thing on earth that I wanted to do."

"I think it's fair to say that I've disrupted your life as well... or at least my father has."

I pressed a wan smile. "I've never been in such a predicament. I mean, I've had to deal with unseemly sorts before. I've had to fight and argue and struggle to get my bounty before. But this..."

A beam of light suddenly illuminated the interior of the garage.

"No," I whispered. "It can't be. It's impossible. Nobody knows about this place."

The ray of light moved across the space; headlights.

"No," I muttered as my heart sank. I didn't want it to be true. I wanted to will it away.

But the sound of tires on gravel confirmed my fears.

"We have to get out of here," Preston said. "Does this old thing work?"

As I slid the key into the ignition, I heard the sound of a slamming car door then quick footsteps as they approached the garage.

Turning the key, I started the car. Despite its bland appearance, the motor purred like a kitten. At least I had that going for me.

"It might be ugly and outdated, but this is the most reliable car I've ever had." I told Preston. "It'll get us to safety.

Chapter 6

Preston

Part of me wanted to switch places with her and take the wheel. I'd done some drag racing in my youth and I knew how to get a car where I wanted it to go and fast.

I felt an overwhelming and urgent need to get her out of there and protect her. It was all I could think about.

But as she flicked the back garage door open, it was clear she knew what she was doing. The garage door slowly cranked its way up just as someone tried to break into the front door.

"Hang on," Priscilla said as she stomped on the accelerator.

The old car shot out of the back door like a bullet. She maneuvered the car through the lot and out to a backstreet.

"Do you know where you're going?" I said as she veered off onto a small street leading us away from the Strip.

"I know this town like the back of my hand. The main arteries, the side streets and the dirt roads that lead out into the desert."

"Yeah, but..." I muttered as we left the city lights and headed west on a dark road.

"Back in San Angelo, you're the boss, but out here..." she said. "Out here I'm in control."

I smiled, inspired by her confidence and her obvious driving abilities.

Thanks to my father, she'd been thrown a curve ball, but she was handling it like a pro. In a split second, she went from lost and confused to knowledgeable and determined.

"Hang on," she called out as she veered onto another dark road.

Smiling, I grabbed onto the door handle and glanced at her. "Remind me to call you if ever I'm in a jam and need a quick getaway."

She pressed on the accelerator, passing cars left and right, all while repeatedly looking in the rearview mirror to make sure we weren't being followed.

"Red Rock Canyon?" I said as I read the sign by the roadside. "Are we going on a camping trip?"

"Not quite," she said with a chuckle. "We're going to Calico Basin."

Well out of the city and with few cars on the road, Priscilla slowed down and let out a relieved breath. "No one behind us for miles," she said. "I think we lost them."

Up ahead I saw the sign indicating the Calico Basin and she turned to the right. The night sky was dimly lit by a sliver of a moon that cast faint shadows all around us.

As she turned to the left, then to the right again, we passed an eclectic variety of homes, many on them large and impressive. Many of them were set far back from the road on generous properties, far from peering eyes.

She turned once again to the right then pulled into a long driveway. "Home, sweet home," she said as she killed the engine.

I looked at the unkept house. Weeds grew high amidst a variety of cacti. One of the small windows was boarded up and the light beside the door hung by its wire.

"Are you sure?" I said. "This place looks abandoned."

She glared at me then looked at her home.

"Hey," I said as I leaned in to try to kiss her. "I didn't mean to offend."

"So, I'm having a little maintenance issue," she said as she backed away from the intended kiss. "I work long hard hours, and I don't have time to tend to that cacti garden. That window got busted by a stray baseball from the neighbor's kid and I haven't been able to get it fixed and, believe it or not, my nine-year-old neighbor thought it would be a good idea to try to hang onto my lamp as he waited for me to answer the door."

"Looks like you need a man around the house."

"Is that an offer?"

She chuckled then stopped just as quickly while her smile faded. Following the direction of her gaze I tried to find what had her so concerned.

"I didn't leave that light on," she said staring at the warm glow coming from a window.

"Are you sure?"

"Positive. Someone's in there."

As she grasped the steering wheel in frustration, a van pulled up to the curb and three men came out.

"What the hell?" Priscilla muttered as she shrunk down in her seat.

I did the same.

The three men walked up to the door.

"They're walked right up as if they own the place." She reached out to open the door, but I quickly grasped her other hand to stop her.

"Wait," I whispered. "Let's wait and see who opens the door."

She nodded as she stared at the door.

The air in the car grew heavy with apprehension as we waited in silence. Then the door finally opened.

"Oh, hell no!" Priscilla spat as she opened the car door. "What the fuck, Tip! You're just letting complete strangers into my house now? Fuck!"

"Priscilla, wait!" I hissed.

But she was already out of the car and stomping her way up to the door. I rushed out of the car and caught her.

"Look at him," she hissed as she struggled to break free of my hold. "What the fuck does he think he's doing?"

"Clearly, he's staying one step ahead of you... of us."

"Well, I'm going to set him straight and get some answers."

"Not now, Pris. This is not the time."

"Really, Preston? You don't think that this is the time to find out what's really going on? Come on."

"We're outnumbered. If we confront them now, we don't stand a chance."

She pulled her gun out. "Outnumbered or not..."

"No," I said more forcefully as I stilled her hands. "We need a plan... a good plan."

Taking in a calming breath, she nodded. "Okay," she said. "You win... for now."

We returned to the car where she started the engine and quietly backed out of the drive.

"Thank you," I said as she turned the corner then crossed the road and went into a large gravel parking lot across the way.

She backed up into a spot and shut off the lights, leaving the engine running.

"What is this place?" I said as I looked around.

"There are trails back there," she said with a dismissive wave at the mountains behind us. "Some rock climbing and stuff."

I looked around, trying to see through the darkness.

"You're right," she said as she stared straight ahead. "We don't have a plan, and we need one."

"Let's review all of this," I said. "Your boss turns up at the Bellagio after our dinner."

"Right."

"With my father's goons who just happen to also show up."

"Right."

"We get away, grab our stuff and head to that garage to hide out."

"Correct."

"And headlights mysteriously appear."

"Also correct."

"So you bring me to your private home."

"Yeah."

"And, what do you know, Tip and three other guys are there."

"Right."

"I don't know about you, but I kind of see a pattern emerging here."

She shot me a cold glare.

"Am I wrong?"

"No," she said. Biting the corner of her lip, she shook her head. "You're right. Too right."

"Any idea how Tip is keeping up with you at every turn?"

"He's a bounty hunter," she said. "I've always thought that he'd shared all his tricks with me, but... I don't know. Maybe he has some additional tricks that he kept to himself."

In the distance, the headlights to the car at her house came on.

"They're on the move again," I said. "Are they going to find us again?"

With a startled gasp, she reached back to the back seat and grabbed her travel bag.

"What are you doing?"

Groaning, she pulled out one item at a time and tossed them to the back seat.

"Priscilla?"

"Aha!" she let out as she pulled up a small coin purse.

"What the hell is that?"

She shot me a sly grin. "A gift from Tip."

I glanced up at the headlights that rounded the corner. They were coming our way.

"They're coming."

Ignoring my comment, she pulled a large pocket knife out of the glove compartment then ripped the lining of the purse open.

"And there we have it," she said as she held up the small tracker.

"Damn," I muttered in disbelief. "So they really have been tracking us."

She handed it to me. "Hang onto this a minute."

Before I could question why, she stepped on the gas and bolted out of the parking lot, passing by the oncoming car.

With breakneck speed, she drove through the sleepy neighborhood, turning the corners with surprising expertise.

We finally emerged onto the main road, and she turned to the right, heading to Red Rock Canyon.

"Give me that thing," she said. "Quick."

As a pick-up truck packed with bales of hay crossed our path, she threw the tracker into the back of the truck.

Impressed, I let out a loud laugh. "You're incredible."

She then spun the car around and pulled over to the side of the road and shut off the headlights.

"What now?" I said.

"We wait," she said, her eyes on the road ahead.

Seconds later a car arrived at the intersection from which we'd emerged. And sure enough, they turned to follow the pick-up truck as it headed into town.

Priscilla finally sank into the driver seat and let out a relieved breath. "Okay. Now I think we're really clear."

"Good. So where do we go now?"

Still looking at the red taillights as they disappeared in the distance, she smiled. "I know this little old ranch that's not far away from here."

Chapter 7

<u>Priscilla</u>

I pulled into the drive of my friend's dude ranch and drove the quarter mile up to her house. To our right, the long narrow structure of the stables stood out, surrounded by corral and a smaller fenced in area.

To our left was the small campground that Gail operated in conjunction with her dude ranch. There were only seven spots and as we neared the main house, I could see a light on in one of the three tiny cabins that she also rented out to guests.

"Nice spread," Preston said as he looked out into the darkness, the moon barely illuminating the impressive property.

"Gail has been running this place for a few years now," I said. I turned off my headlights and pulled up in front of the house. "She has a real head for business, and a heart as big as Texas, but..." I quietly got out of the car and looked into the dark house. "Well, I don't know how she's going to take my coming here so late in the night."

Before I could close the car door, I heard one of her dogs bark, then a light in the living room came on and seconds later the door opened. Gail stood there in her nightgown, her shotgun in hand.

"You'd better have a dang good reason to be comin' up my drive this time of night. I'm not expecting any new guest."

"Gail," I said cautiously. "It's me. Priscilla."

"Priscilla?" she said as she lowered the shotgun. "Damn, girl. Why didn't you let me know? Hell, are you in trouble?"

I went around the car and walked up to her, eager to put my head to her shoulder. Her dog, reassured that all was well, went back inside.

"Talk to me, honey," Gail said as she pulled me in for a big mama bear hug. "What's going on?"

She was a big and strong woman with a shock of white hair and an angry scowl when trouble was in the air. But when a friend was in need, she opened her arms and gave them all the support and love they needed.

And I needed.

"I'm sorry for showing up like this," I said. "But I'm exhausted. It's a long sordid and complicated story. All I can say for now is that we've had one hell of a night."

"We?"

I turned back to the car where Preston still sat and waved him over.

He opened the door and stepped out, quickly drawing an impressed sigh from Gail.

"Oh, honey," she whispered to me as Preston made his way over. "That's nice. Real nice. That's the sort of trouble that I can really appreciate."

I smiled as she immediately shot her hand out to grasp his.

"Gail Bowden," she said as she vigorously shook Preston's hand.

"Nice to meet you," he said. "I'm Preston Prickly, Priscilla's friend."

"Well, any friend of Priscilla's is certainly welcomed in my home. You kids come on in."

She gestured for Preston to walk in ahead of us. As he did so, she glanced at me, smiled, cocked her brow and gave me a silent thumbs up.

Leaning into her, we walked in behind Preston and headed into the living room.

"This is a very lovely home you have, Miss Bowden," Preston said.

The large rustic home was warm with caramel colored wood, stone floor in the kitchen and wrought iron trimmings.

Gail waved Preston's comment away. "First off, this is just your average, homey, comfy, kick-off-your-boots sort of house, and that's the way I like it. Secondly, the name is Gail. And if you don't mind, I'm gonna go right ahead and call you Preston."

"You do that, ma'am," Preston said with a boyish grin.

"Do you have many guests this week?"

She began counting on her fingers. "I have an older couple from Massachusetts, a younger family from Arizona and two macho men from Tennessee." She looked up at me. "And I'm expecting four more wannabe cowboys this weekend."

"Business is good, I see."

"Better than expected," she said. "People want to get outdoors and enjoy the fresh air. Aint no better way than to get on the back of a horse and head out into the Nevada desert."

"I can sure appreciate that," Preston said.

Gail turned to me. "You kids want some coffee? A snack? I can whip up some…"

"I appreciate it, Gail," I said, putting my hand to her shoulder. "Like I said, we're exhausted. I really just want to get cleaned up and hit the sack."

"Well, I won't lie and say I'm disappointed. I'm kinda eager to go back to bed myself. You kids head out to the guest house. You know the way, don't you?"

"Sure do."

"I'll go out and get our bags," Preston offered as he headed to the door.

"Oh," I said softly. "Right."

The moment he walked out, Gail turned to me.

"He certainly is a handsome man, if ever I saw one."

"That, he is."

"And he certainly seems to have a sweet disposition."

I smiled. "He has his moments."

94

"Oh, Priscilla," she said. "I'm so happy to see you with a man. You deserve a good, strong man."

I guffawed. "Gail!"

"What? You do. You've been alone for so long. Far, far too long."

"I have you, don't I?" I said with a teasing grin.

Although she was only fifteen years older than me, she was very much a mother figure in my life, always ready to open her heart and share her wisdom.

"You are young, and beautiful, and smart and you deserve a good man who is going to be able to appreciate all that you have to offer."

As Preston returned, I kissed Gail goodnight and led him out the back door and headed to the small guesthouse a hundred yards behind the main house.

"She's quite a character," Preston said as we walked side by side. His voice was beginning to show signs of fatigue.

"Gail? Yeah. She's a great person. Incredible. I knew you'd like her. She doesn't have a pretentious bone in her body, so what you see is what you get. If she's happy with you, she'll let you know. And if she's not, well, she's likely to let you know even faster."

We reached the guesthouse, and I opened the door to let us in.

"Cute," Preston said as he took a look around the one-room house. "Quaint."

The large room was well divided into four quadrants; bedroom, living space, kitchen and dining area, with a closed off portion at the back for a small bathroom.

An old style four-poster bed was set up in one corner, with a tall dresser serving as a divider between it and the small living space. The red and clack checkered sofa had its back to the dining area which was essentially part of the kitchen that was small but well designed, making it highly functional.

"I've always loved this place," I said as I moved to the center of the small space and looked around.

Preston peeled off his shirt, kicked off his boots and rid himself of his pants. "I'm hitting the shower."

I watched him head to the only door in the house, successfully finding the bathroom without even asking.

Slowly taking off my clothes, I finally allowed myself to breathe, to really breathe. It had been an exhausting day, and I was emotionally drained as well as physically.

But as I made my way to the bathroom, I knew that we were safe in this secluded part of Las Vegas.

I joined Preston in the shower. My tense muscles instantly relaxed under the warm water, and as Preston lathered me up, tears of release sprang to my eyes.

"You okay?" he said as he noticed my reddening eyes.

"Overwhelmed," I said simply.

He gently washed me with his hands, rinsed off the soap then turned off the water. He reached for a big fluffy towel and patted me dry, never once eluding to anything sexual.

"Come on," he said as he picked me up and carried me to the bed where we were both out like a light.

*****

"I don't really want to know what's going on or what brought you here," Gail said. "But I do want you to know that you can stay here as long as you need to."

"Thanks," I said.

Seated on her large back patio, I sipped my coffee, looking out at the simple yet rewarding life that Gail had carved out for herself.

She had a stable filled with magnificent horses and scattered around the property were several goats and two cows. Her three dogs, Boxer, Fighter and Killer, ensured the security of the place while her two cats, Fluff and Ball made sure that the mice population was kept under control. She had dozens of chickens running around the place.

While horseback riding was a large portion of her business, whenever she had families with kids come around, they enjoyed the various animals that they could feed and pet.

It was an enviable life.

The air was quiet, still, with only the cluck of the chickens in the distance.

"I just got a new Appaloosa," Gail said, breaking the silence. "He's a dandy. Tall, proud and very selective about who he'll let on his back."

"I'd love to go for a ride this afternoon, if you don't mind."

"You always had a soft spot for Breeze."

I chuckled as I nodded. "I don't know what it is about Pintos. They're just such terrific animals. Is Breeze too old to ride now?"

Her smile faded as she looked at me with somber eyes. "I'm sorry, honey. I thought I'd already told you. We lost Breeze last spring."

I smiled despite the loss and reached out to pat Gail's hand. "That animal was destined to the glue factory when you found him," I said. "You gave him a wonderful life... wonderful years of fresh air, clean stable and plenty of loving attention. I may not know horse speak, but every time I came here and saw him, he always seemed happy... as happy as a horse can demonstrate."

The slamming of a door brought my attention to the distant guesthouse. Preston, in jeans and a crisp white shirt embroidered with black at the shoulder, was heading our way.

Fighter, a border collie, immediately jumped to her feet and headed out to greet him, while Boxer and Killer barely glanced at him. Two old bloodhounds, they chose to lay back and let Fighter escort Preston.

"Speaking of wonderful animals," Gail said. "Wherever did you find that fine specimen of a man?"

His stride was so cool, so sexy... so easy... so...

Mine?

I ignored the fluttering of my heart and smiled at Gail. "He's from San Angelo," I said.

She looked at me in surprise. "Texas?"

"That's the one."

"Well, I'll be damned. Guess I'm gonna have to take a trip to Texas and find myself a beast like him."

I playfully slapped her arm as I laughed. She was an incredible flirt, always cracking jokes about men and relationships.

"Good morning, ladies," Preston said as he came up the steps to the patio.

"Good morning, Preston," Gail said. "Coffee?"

He nodded. Squinting, he looked out at the horses grazing nearby. "Is that a Arabian horse?"

"It is indeed," Gail said. "You know your horses."

"I was hoping to go for a ride this afternoon, if you're up for it," I said.

"Sounds great." He looked at his watch. "Afternoon is going to come around quick. We got a late start to the day."

Gail pushed her chair back and stood. "You kids enjoy your coffee. I'm gonna go inside and fix you a full breakfast then you can go for that ride and be back in time for a good old country-style homecooked meal out back at the campground."

*****

By the time we returned from our ride, the ranch was bustling with activity.

"I don't know what she's cooking out there, but it sure smells good," Preston said.

"She usually has Rich Landau come out to handle the grill and all. He's a well-known cook out here in Nevada."

"Well, my stomach is eager to try out his food."

I nodded my agreement, and we led the horses inside the stable. "I hope you don't mind us staying here for a few days," I said as I got down from an old quarter horse that was as docile as could be.

Our ride had been quiet and introspective, neither one of us willing to bring up the events of the night before.

Preston nodded. "A few days is fine," he said. "But I am going to have to check in with things back home."

"Sure." I removed the bridle from my horse then reached under her belly to unbuckle the saddle. Before I could remove it, Preston came up behind me and deftly removed the heavy Western saddle and set it on the rack. "Thanks," I said.

He winked and my knees turned to mush.

I was surprised by how well he was taking this unexpected turn of events. He was patient and understanding, but I couldn't help but wonder if pent up anger was brewing underneath that handsome grin of his.

We took our time tending to the horses, almost reluctant to leave the solace and quiet of the stables.

"Ready?" I said when the horses were back in the stalls, content with their fresh water and handful of oats.

Rubbing his belly, he smiled. "Sure am."

We headed out to the crowd, mingling with many of Gail's guests as we enjoyed fresh baked beans, perfectly grilled steaks, and a spread that could have fed a crowd twice the size as she had.

When we finished our meal, Preston went around picking up empty plates, stacking up empty cups all while smiling and chatting with the guests.

"Can I keep him?" Gail said with a grin.

We stood on the perimeter of the crowd, watching everyone enjoying themselves. With my can of beer in hand, I laughed and leaned into her.

"I'm not even sure if I can keep him," I said.

"Oh?"

"He's a very strong-minded, independent type of guy. Besides… San Angelo. That's a long way away." I looked at her. "Did I tell you that he has a ranch?"

"A dude ranch?"

"No. A sheep ranch."

"Oh! No. You didn't tell me that."

"A very successful sheep ranch. He supplies high quality wool to a number of… well, I don't know. Knitters, I guess."

She burst out laughing. "Oh, Priscilla."

I laughed at my own silliness, then sobered up as I watched Preston getting on with everyone. "He's good with people," I said. "But I'm sure he misses his ranch back home."

As people began to disperse, Gail and I walked over to her back porch and sat down. It'd been a long and satisfying day.

"Look at him," Gail said, pointing her can of beer at Preston who was carrying two large garbage bags to the garbage bin. "He just never stops."

I pressed a sad smile as I watched him disappear around the corner of the house. Was he just being nice and courteous, or was he desperate to keep busy in order to avoid thinking about everything that was going on?

"I think he's used to being busy back home. He's not the kind of guy to sit back and relax much."

He returned moments later, his phone to his ear.

"... glad to hear it," he was saying as he approached us. "I knew I could rely on you guys. But I want you to keep your eyes open. I'm having issues with my biological father. I think that he might show up at the ranch." He nodded and shook his head as he listened. "Seriously, Bacon. Don't take this lightly. My dad's not exactly a stand-up citizen, if you know what I mean."

He was silent for a long moment as he listened. "Yeah," he said. "I'm still out here in Vegas. It's a bit fucked up, but we had somebody tailing us last night. If anyone does come around the house, don't tell them anything about where we are. Yeah... I think it could be dangerous. We'll lie low... and you guys be careful."

Chapter 8

__Priscilla__

The final glow of daylight was all that was left as Preston and I left Gail and headed to our tiny little home away from home.

"You really impressed Gail," I said, resisting the urge to reach out and hold his hand as we walked side by side.

"Really? How's that?"

"You know… being so sweet to everyone, taking me out for a horseback ride, helping to pick up after that huge cook-out… all that."

"Well, the horseback ride was fun. You know, I didn't realize that Las Vegas could be so beautiful. All I knew about the town was that it was full of casinos, flashy shows and that the deserts were filled with dead gangsters buried here and there or something like that. But out here... it almost feels like home." He looked at me. "Almost."

"I know you must be eager to get back home, but..."

"Don't worry about it. I can handle a few days away. Besides, it'll give my guys a chance to really prove themselves to me... not that they need to."

"Hey," I said as we arrived at the guesthouse. "Since you like the scenery out here so much, how about a midnight ride?"

He glanced at his watch. "But it's only ten o'clock."

I stopped walking and turned to face him. Jutting out my hip, I tilted my head to the side and poked my tongue into my cheek. "Cute. You think you're funny, don't you?"

With a crooked grin, he shrugged. "Sometimes."

God, he was adorable. I was amazed every time I saw that boyish look in his eyes, that look that erased the hard edge he could sometimes have when he was angry or concentrated on something.

"Well, Mr. Smartass. Do you want to go for that ride, or do you want to argue about the time?"

"Lead the way," he said, his hand coming up to briefly caress my shoulder.

We walked to the stable and got the same two horses we'd ridden on earlier. But as Preston reached for a saddle, I stopped him.

"This is just a casual little ride," I said. "Bareback."

"Oh. I do believe that will be a first," he said.

"What? A man from Texas who has never ridden bareback? I don't believe you."

He laughed. "When I was twelve, I rode a sheep bareback. Does that count?"

It was my turn to laugh. I pulled a woolen blanket off its hook and wrapped it around my shoulders to ward off the chill of night that I knew would soon fall upon us. The I turned and guided my horse outside. "Come on. Enough with the chatter."

Once outside we climbed onto the horses' backs and veered off to the right, taking a trail that led up a rocky hill that lined the back portion of Gail's ranch.

"So, where are we exactly?" Preston said as we began to climb the hill and our surroundings slowly came into view.

"The less you know, the better," I said, glancing back at him.

"Are you sure your boss doesn't know about this place?" he said.

My heart pounded suddenly as I had a moment of doubt. I tried to quickly go through various conversations I had with Tip over the years. Had I ever mentioned Gail?

Possibly.

Had I mentioned the nature of my relationship with her?

I couldn't see why I would have, but… maybe.

Had I ever told him of Gail's ranch and its location?

No. I was certain I hadn't.

Still, an uncomfortable chill settled onto my shoulders and I pulled the blanket closer around me.

"Are you okay?" Preston said through the gentle clopping of our horses' hooves.

"Huh?" I said, wondering why he would ask.

"You grunted," he said. "You okay?"

Was my pain and discomfort with the Tip situation to the point where it was audible?

Wow. I really had to do something to calm me… really calm me down. Despite the paradisiacal surroundings, despite the cool demeanor I displayed… Damn it. I was still wound up inside.

Prick*ly Promise (Prickly Proposal #2)

We arrived at the top of the rocky hill and turned the horses to face Gail's ranch down below us. In the distance stood Charleston Peak, its perennial cap of snow glistening in the moonlight.

My horse neighed and whinnied while tapping the ground with his front hoof.

Without saying anything, I shrugged off the blanket letting it drape over the horse's backside, then slid off his back. Preston looked at me for a moment before getting down from his horse. He stood near me, looking out into the desert.

My skin tingled with the hunger for his touch.

Still without saying anything, I reached for his hand. He turned to look at me and I leaned into him, kissing him with a strange determination that surprised me.

I pulled him to me, ready to devour him.

For a tortured moment, he didn't reciprocate. No doubt this rollercoaster ride that we were on was hard on him. Was sex not an option?

The night before, in the shower… while he'd been tender and loving, he'd washed me. Simply washed me. He hadn't lingered on my breasts, he hadn't sought to delve between my legs, and he hadn't caressed my buttocks.

Nothing. Was the electricity between us already dead?

Just as I was about to pull back, he wrapped his arms around me and returned the kiss with pent up anger, frustration and passion.

With curled fingers, he pulled up my skirt and grasped my ass cheeks, kneading the eager flesh as he groaned.

As our kiss became increasingly heated and all consuming, we staggered back until I was leaning against my horse who swung his head around to look at us as he snorted loudly.

Through the ongoing kiss, Preston chuckled. "Critiqued by a horse," he muttered. "That's a first."

I managed to find the presence of mind to pull away from the heated kiss. Turning to the horse, I pulled off the thick wool blanket.

Through hooded eyes, Preston looked at me with a horny grin on his face. "I like the way you think… even at a time like this you're pragmatic."

I unfurled the blanket and set it on the ground in front of the horses.

"Yeah," Preston said, still apparently dazed by my sudden and passionate onslaught. "You really are pragmatic and smart."

Wrapping my hand around to the back of his neck, I once again pulled him into a passionate kiss, all while guiding him down to the blanket.

"Are you not bothered by the horses looking down on us?" he said as I straddled him and peeled off my shirt.

"You talk too much," I said. With my breasts freed of my constrictive push up bra, I fell over him, crushing my breasts to his chest as my tongue poured into his mouth.

His hardened bulge pressed against me as I grinded into him.

"Enough dry humping," he said. He grabbed me by the waist and flipped me onto my back, then quickly threw off his boots and his jeans. As an afterthought, he removed his shirt.

Naked and glorious, he came to me, his erection so huge and hard, I thought he might climax right there before even touching me again.

With a quick motion, he yanked off my underwear then nestled between my legs.

"It's been a while," he growled as he entered me.

"In the shower... our first night here..." I mumbled incoherently, already flying off on the sensations.

"That was a quick welcome to Las Vegas fuck," he said as he slowly pulled out only to take his time as he pushed back in. "Tonight, under the stars, with Sin City out there somewhere, I want to savor you. I want to take my time and enjoy the feel of your skin, the smell of your hair and the…"

"Still talking too much," I blurted out as I grabbed his butt cheeks, tilted one side of my hip up, effectively pushing him off me and onto his back.

With my breasts hovering just above his face, I climbed onto him. "This is my town," I said. "I take the lead. I tell you when and where… and how."

A strange and satisfied grin spread over his lips as he interlaced his fingers and brought his hands under his head. Biting his lower lip, he looked at me, his eyes intense, almost dark.

I lay over him, kissing his nipple as my hand caressed his raging cock.

"I certainly do like your way of doing things," he said.

I lightly trailed my hands over his chest as I nudged my way down until his stiff erection was in my face.

Preston pulled in a tight breath of anticipation, but I kept him waiting. I gently caressed the member with my fingers, then set a chaste kiss on the very tip.

"Are you trying to drive me crazy?" he said. He'd removed his hands from under his head and now clenched the blanket on either side of him.

"Is it working?" I whispered

He grunted. "Damn right, it is."

I pulled him into my mouth, slowly taking him all in. Once I had him, I ran my tongue around then slowly drew back.

"Damn, Priscilla," he said with a sigh.

"I can stop if it's too excruciating."

"Don't you dare," he whispered through his teeth as he brought his hands to my head, his fingers digging into my scalp, unequivocally suggesting that I dive back in.

I continued on, slow and torturous, drawing a heaving breath with every pull on his cock.

"Ready?" I said as I pulled away from his cock and came up to his face.

"Hell, yeah."

"You sure?" I grabbed his cock in a tight fist and worked him up.

"Oh, yeah."

"Real sure?"

"Yes. Yes!"

I pumped my fist faster and tighter all while clamping down over his mouth with mine, delving in to meet his tongue.

His muffled cries echoed in my mouth as the first pounding throb of his cock registered the oncoming orgasm to my hand. I pressed my lips tighter over his, refusing to allow him to cry out. He struggled under me, and his body shook. His cock pounded in my hand, like a heartbeat… ready to explode.

"Ah," he managed to let out through the kiss.

The remainder of his climatic cries were contained in my mouth as his body went rigid. I held him captive until his body finally recovered from the orgasm.

"Hot damn," he said with a long exhale.

Both horses whinnied loudly, and Preston tilted his head back and laughed.

"Under the stars, out in the desert, and with a chorus of horses," he said through his laughter. "You sure do know how to give a guy a new and unexpected experience."

I sat up to straddle him, looking down at him and wondering what we were. We were both behaving as if we needed to continue with the charade of being engaged. Then again, he had introduced himself to Gail as a friend. Had I been quick enough to make the introduction, would I have done the same?

Was it a fact? Were we just friends? Or no. Even worst. We weren't friends. We were embroiled in a strange and unusual... what? Relationship? Business? Chase?

Prick*ly Promise (Prickly Proposal #2)

Or were we simply lovers taking advantage of the unusual circumstances?

Chapter 9

Preston

I woke up to an empty bed and instantly wondered where Priscilla was. Then, as I sat up, I saw a note tucked under the glass of orange juice that was set on the nearby dining table.

Checking my watch, I was surprised to find that it was well past ten. "That girl is making a soft old man of you."

With an amused chuckle, I got out of bed, my cock still stiff due to vivid dreams of the night before. I pulled on a pair of jeans, thinking of just how perfect she was. Her touch, her tongue, the crush of her breasts against me.

We were still behaving as if we in the charade of being engaged, but why? Because it suited us, I thought. And it certainly did.

I pulled on a tight white t-shirt and my boots, drank down the orange juice in one gulp and headed out to the main house.

While the air wasn't stifling, the heat of the day was already on, reminding me very much of Texas.

Don't even go there, I told myself, unwilling to let myself get homesick.

I reached the main house and could hear some pleasant humming coming from inside. I opened the door a crack as saw just enough of Priscilla's face to see that the musical sound was coming from her.

Then I entered.

Walking into the house was like walking into a decorating store. Ribbons were twirled into various types of bows, tall bouquets of decorative branches stood in large white vases and Priscilla and

Gail were at a long working table twisting together tiny flowers to make tiny bouquets.

"What's all this?" I said, noticing the smell of bacon as I looked around.

Priscilla fell silent and both women looked up at me and smiled.

"Well, there you are," Priscilla said. "I was beginning to think that all this desert air was a little too much for you."

"Never," I said with a snort.

"You're a little late for breakfast," Gail said, tilting her head toward the long dining room table that still had goodies spread out. "But there's still plenty left."

"Good," I said as I patted my stomach. "I'm starving."

But instead of going to the dining room table, I came up to them to take a closer look at what they were doing. Picking up one of the miniature bouquets, I looked at Priscilla.

"Gail occasionally holds weddings here," she said. "There's going to be a big one next week and I thought I'd help her get a few of the little things ready."

"On the day before and of the wedding," Gail said. "I'm far too busy with other things… like cooking for dozens of people."

"If we're here long enough," Priscilla said. "I might even help with the wedding cake. I love decorating cakes."

"Well," I said as I turned and headed to the table that held far more interesting items. "I'd love to help you gals out, but…" I picked up a strip of bacon and took a bite. Nothing in the world is better than bacon.

"Everything that's there is all yours," Gail called out to me. "My guests have already eaten and many of them are gone or getting ready to leave."

I scooped up some scrambled eggs and set in the middle of a big piece of homemade bread then slapped two slices of bacon on top. Folding the overstuffed slice of bread, I grabbed a plate to keep from making a mess and took a big bite as I headed back to the table where the girls were working.

"Keep that slop away from my flowers, now," Gail said, her hand popping out to keep me from getting any closer.

"Slop?" I said. "But this is your food."

"When I'm preparing for a wedding as big as this one is going to be, any bite of food that comes around in this vicinity is slop, as far as I'm concerned."

I snorted and took a few steps back. "Yes, ma'am."

Priscilla bit down on an amused smile as she continued to put together those tiny bouquets.

"What else is there to prepare?" I said through my mouthful.

"I have napkins to fold."

"Now?" I said. "Isn't it a bit too soon for that?"

"The bride wants a very specific way of folding them. I can't wait until the last day," Gail said. "Then I have dozens of small white vases that the bride wants painted hot pink and orange."

I grimaced as I took a bite of my breakfast.

"Then we have all the place cards to write... you know... the names of all the guests," she said, pointing to a small white box of blank place cards. "All hundred and twelve of them."

"I could do them," I said.

Both women looked up at me.

"You?" Priscilla said.

"No offence, Preston, dear," Gail said. "But those place cards require... well... a delicate, and even romantic..."

"Calligraphy?" I finished for her as I popped the last bite of my breakfast into my mouth.

"Yes," she said. "Exactly."

After wiping my hands off on a paper napkin, I went to the small box and picked up a card.

"Preston," Priscilla said, her tone carrying a hint of a warning.

I picked up the pen that was laid over the guest list.

Gail, gaping and wide-eyed, looked on.

"Belinda Barsky," I said, reading the first name on the list.

With a beautiful and elegant flourish, I wrote the name on the card, then slipped it over to Gail.

She picked up the card and stared at it. "Well, I'll be damned."

"Is it good?" Priscilla said.

Gail passed the card to her. "It's perfect."

Priscilla looked at the card, then up at me, then back at the card. "Where did you learn to do this?"

I simply smiled, and when she looked up at me once again, I could see a whole new level of admiration in her eyes.

"So…" I said.

"The job is yours if you want it."

"Sure," I said as I picked up the box and sat at the end of the table with them.

*****

"If you were looking to impress Gail," Priscilla said as we strolled through the now empty campground. "You've succeeded, and then some."

I'd finished half of the place cards while they'd finished with the bouquets. "I was happy to help."

"Well, you know, now that you've done half of them, you have to do the rest. She can't have two different handwritings on those cards."

I looked at her, wondering if someone would really make a fuss if place cards didn't have the same handwriting, but I didn't argue the point.

After all, what did I know about weddings and all the details they involved.

"I'll do the rest of them after lunch."

"Thanks. I'm sure Gail will appreciate it."

I shrugged. "And what will you be doing?"

She stopped walking suddenly and turned to face me. "This morning, while you slept, I checked up on Tip."

"Checked up? What do you mean? I thought we were hiding from him."

"I have my own little way of tracking Tip. Because we were once so close, we had a way of keeping track of one another through our phones… even at Tip's office."

"Okay," I said. "And what did you find out?"

"Well, for one thing, Tip hasn't returned to his office," she said. "I took a look at the security cameras back at the office and there has been no activity." She looked up at me. "He's still out there actively looking for us."

I shook my head. "Can't say that I'm surprised."

"I know that this is a major inconvenience for you," she went on. "But we'll have to remain in hiding for a while longer. I know that we're safe here, and Gail has invited us to stay as long as we need."

I nodded, thinking of all the work I had waiting for me back home. As competent and hard working as my guys were, there were aspects of the business that I had to tend to personally.

As I plunged my fists into my pockets, Priscilla walked over to the remains of a campfire that still smoked. With a quick flick of her boot, she tossed sand over the dying ambers and snuffed out the fire. She ambled around the campsite, her lips drawn down and her brow furrowed.

She was worried about my reaction to this news. I could almost see her stress level rising with every breath. Since leaving the house, she'd grown fidgety, avoided eye contact with me and looked around nervously at every little sound.

"I guess there are worse places to be," I said, trying to lighten her mood.

She stopped and looked at me, pressing a tight and uncertain smile as her eyes remained lost and confused.

"And I guess there are worse people that I could be stuck with."

Her smile broadened, reaching her eyes and warming her face.

"Come on," I said, holding my hand out to her. "Let's go back to the house and show Gail just how much we appreciate her hospitality."

As we walked back to the house, I felt her relax. Her stride was calm and slow. Then, out of nowhere, she leaned into me and looked up into my eyes.

"Do you think you could show me a bit of that calligraphy stuff that you do?"

***

With Gail's wedding preparations all taken care of, Priscilla and I headed out to the stable. We worked in quiet harmony, cleaning stalls, brushing horses and putting away saddles and other riding gear.

The pace over the next few days was peaceful and simple. We rose early in the morning, ate a good breakfast and worked a good part of the day.

But as I looked at Priscilla, busy feeding the chickens, I wondered how long we could hide out.

As if reading my mind, she looked at me.

How long did we have?

Chapter 10

<u>Jackson Prickly</u>

"What the fuck is going on?" I shouted at Tip. Sitting at my granite-topped desk in my office, I looked at him over the tip of my cigar.

Shit, he'd turned out to be a disappointment. I'd invested so much time in him and now he was letting me down in a major way.

He looked at me. I could see the gears working in that little head of his. He was trying to find a way to appease me.

Well, keep trying, I wanted to say. *Yeah Keep trying.*

"Everything will fall into place," Tip said blinking wildly from under his sweaty brow. "You'll see."

"Everything was supposed to fall into place yesterday, Greene. That's what you said, right? What the fuck? Stop making excuses for this girl of yours. Your little Priscilla screwed up. She screwed up big time. She's your protégé and you're responsible for her actions... and her actions are speaking quite clearly. She's fucked you over. Face it. Deal with it. Fix it!"

"Look," he said, barely able to look at me. "We are where we are and there's little I can do about it now. But I promise that..."

"Fuck your promises! All the bitch had to do was schmooze up to that bastard son of mine and get his ass over here," I shouted. "I thought you said that she was a pro."

"She is."

"And you told me that this girl trusted you."

"She does... or she did," he said. But uncertainty played in his eyes. He was no longer sure what his relationship with that girl was.

"And I even sent you back up by sending in two of my men... two of my best men."

He steepled his fingers and tapped the points of his index fingers against his chin.

"Damn it, Tip. That fucking blonde bimbo is messing with you."

He clucked his tongue out and took a nervous sip of the high-end bourbon I'd offered him.

I looked at him, scrutinized him. He hated coming to my office. I could see it in his eyes. The fear. The uncertainty. Shit, I could almost smell the disdain on his skin. But I didn't give a fuck. He had a job to do, and I wanted it done.

Then again, there was the occasional flicker of envy in the old bugger's eyes.

Don't forget, Tip Greene. I'm the one with the money. I'm the one with the power. I know what I want, and I know how to get it.

136

"Priscilla is a beautiful girl," he said, cautiously taking her defense. "And that beauty can be quite disarming."

"No shit," I said. I put my cigar out in the ashtray that was carved out of stone. Leering at him, I stood. "That bitch has wasted enough of my time."

"She's smarter than people give her credit for," Tip said. "They see a flashy blonde and think there's nothing in her head... but I can tell you... there's plenty in there. She analyses things. She sees things that others don't notice."

I slammed my palm onto my massive desk, almost tipping over his fucking glass of bourbon. "I don't give a fuck! Did I ask you for her resumé? No! Don't fucking waste my time telling me about the girl who is out here – God knows where – with my son... My son! And I want him here."

"I'm just saying that she must have figured out that Preston was in danger."

I waved his comment away and turned to look out the window that overlooked the busy Strip down below. "If this girl of yours is so smart," I said, working fucking hard to keep my calm. "Do you think she knows what happened to her father?"

He shrugged. "Don't think so." He looked up at me. "Do you think Pinkerton knows that you had him framed for grand larceny?"

I let out a loud, bellowing laugh. "What the fuck do you think?" I said as I picked a fresh cigar from the humidor I kept on the console behind my desk. "Of course not. The fucker is so holier than thou. Shit. I've never seen a guy be so fucking honest. His fucking mother probably taught him how noble it was to be good and honest. Shit. I hate women like that. You know what that does? Huh? Do you?"

He shook his head and watched me clip off the tip of my cigar.

"It fucking makes little lambs out of the fuckers. Little lambs that are so easily brought to slaughter."

"How'd you manage it?" he said.

I chuckled.

"One of his managers – a dweeb looking kind of guy named Chris Abbots – was one of my guys. He did a real fine job getting into Pinkertons books, his numbers, his deals, and contracts. Once he was in, it was child's play."

"So, Pinkerton went to prison for something that this Chris guy did?"

"Damn right, he did. And that's where he's going to stay for a good long while still." I pointed my unlit cigar at him. "I can promise you that."

Tip swirled the bourbon around in his glass then took a sip. His hands shook. His brow beaded with sweat. He was practically pissing in his boots. Yeah. I had the guy squirming, all right.

Still pointing my cigar at him, I squinted at him and headed back to my chair to sit down. "You know, Tip. That's the thing I like about you. You're a pragmatic guy, aren't you? You don't fuck around. You get the job done… and you know how much your reputation is worth. You don't fuck around on the side. You don't fuck around behind my back. You just shut your trap and do the fucking job, right?"

He nodded.

I lit my cigar and puffed smoke into his face. "You don't waste time judging your clients, do you? No. Why would you? I fucking feed you. But that fucking chick of yours…" I pointed my cigar at him. "She has a few lessons to learn, you know what I mean?"

He nodded again, sweat dripping off his brow, down his cheek and off his chin onto his swampy shirt.

"Chicks like her are too easy to buy. You know that for a fact, don't you?"

"Priscilla wouldn't stab me in the back like that," he said, sure of himself.

"Right. Like no other chick has ever stabbed a guy in the back before. Fucking Christ. Chicks are bought every fucking day of the week. You buy them dinner. You buy them flowers. You fucking throw down a few grand for some fucking rock that is going to make her all giddy and feeling special like shit."

He wiped the sweat from his brow with his nasty hanky that he pulled out of his pant pocket.

I leaned over my desk and looked him in the eye. "It's a dog-eat-dog world out there, Greene. Everybody turns on everybody some time or other."

"Look," he said. "She's smart and she knows her way around. But she doesn't have my experience. I mean, I taught her a lot of tricks of the trade, but... well, I kept a few of those secrets to myself, you know. I'll fix this."

"Well, I'm happy to hear that you have some sense."

He pressed a wry grin. "I'll find her. Don't you worry. I'll find her... and I'll get her bounty."

"Fucking right, you will. If not, everyone in Vegas will be after that bitch."

"What are you saying?" Tip said, his eyes suddenly hooded with questions and doubts.

"I can't waste any more time on this. I've sent a message out."

"What kind of message?"

"One that will get everyone off their fucking asses. One that will have everyone looking for that blonde bimbo and that half-assed son of mine."

He looked at me, waiting for me to go on.

"My message will have every bounty hunters out there on high alert. The guy who brings me Preston and his fucking bitch... six figures, Tip." I held up all fingers of one hand and the thumb of the other. "I've offered six figures to any bounty hunter who brings me my son to me. Think anyone will bite?"

He nodded. "With money like that," he murmured, "it's sure to get everyone's attention."

Chapter 11

Tip

Jackson was one hell of a character, and as I left his office I wondered what he had in store for Priscilla and Preston. How far would he go?

I had no clue.

Priscilla was my charge… my protégé… my responsibility. And I had every intention of setting things right with her. She had to understand the consequences of her actions.

I drove back to my office trying to plot out my next move. Since Priscilla had so deftly thrown me off her track, I had to find another way of getting to her.

But how.

Shit, she was smart… too smart for her own good sometimes. And this might very well be the time that all of this bites her on the ass.

I walked into my office. It looked like a closet compared to Jackson's, but as compact as it was, it was nice and airy. And while I didn't have his spectacular view of the Strip, I had a decent view of Lone Mountain in the distance… that is, if I stood and looked over the top of some of the nearby buildings.

Now what?

I grabbed the bottle of cheap whiskey that I kept in the filing cabinet and took a swig.

"This crap is just as good as that dirtbag's expensive stuff." So expensive that he'd barely poured a few drops into my glass before handing it to me... the fucking cheapskate.

I sat at my desk and swiveled around to look out the window. Kicking my feet up onto the windowsill, I took another swig of whiskey.

This whole crappy affair was falling apart, and I could feel the wave of panic settling in. I couldn't let that happen. I had to keep a cool head.

"Come on, Tip," I said. "Get it together and fix this thing."

I looked at my phone as if there was an answer in there somewhere. Finding her. Tracking her. Getting her to fucking smarten up and bring Preston to his father. That was what I had to do.

How, Tip? Think. Think!

Where had she found him?

San Angelo.

And what was out there?

I smiled. A ranch. His ranch. His pride and joy. What would Preston Prickly do to save his ranch?

Well, hell. If Priscilla was able to find this precious ranch of his, I could find it as well. Planning my trip, I poured more whiskey. My plan was coming together. Yeah... more whiskey.

I fell asleep in my chair with thoughts of my plan on my mind and the moment I woke up, my mouth dry and my head aching, I put away the nearly emptied bottle of whiskey and headed out.

The sun was just coming over the horizon as I got into my car and turned in the direction of San Angelo, Texas.

I made it out of Nevada quick enough, but Arizona was a chore to get through with New Mexico not much better. The sun was preparing to go down behind me as I crossed over into Texas.

"Think you're smart, little girl," I muttered into my brand-new Buick. "Well, this old fart has been at this game a lot longer than you have. No matter what you do, I'll outplay you every single time."

Chapter 12

Priscilla

"How many cookouts have you prepared this year so far, Gail?" I said as I snapped the heads off of a pile of green beans.

"I think I just might go crazy if I stop and count them all," she said with a chuckle. "Don't get me wrong, love. This ranch is my life and I feel blessed each and every day. But there are days when these old legs don't want to walk as quickly as I would like them to. And there are those days when my back keeps reminding me that I need to slow down just a little, teeny bit. But..."

She glanced out the kitchen window and I followed the direction of her gaze.

Preston, on Gail's brand-new Appaloosa, was returning from a ride out in the desert.

"Dang it," she muttered. "That man is going to know that horse better than I do."

"I think he's taken the liberty of naming him," I said with a grin. "Ralph, I believe."

"Ralph? On, dear. That's no name for a horse."

I let out a light laugh.

I'd grown accustomed to the laid-back type of life that ranch living offered. Yeah, the work was hard – physically demanding. But damn it was rewarding.

Preston brought the horse around the back patio and slid off the saddle. Seconds later, he pushed the door open and came in to join us.

"Are you just going to leave my horse there?" Gail said, a little perplexed.

"Ralph?" Preston said, a little nonchalant as he came to my pile of green beans, picked one up and took a bite.

148

"I was thinking of calling him Blaze," Gail said. "And I don't want him wandering around the yard willy-nilly like that."

"He won't go anywhere," Preston said with all the confidence of someone who knew his horse. "And I really think that Ralph suits him."

Charmed, Gail just smiled and nodded. "Fine. You win. Ralph it is."

"Smells good in here," he said as he raked his fingers through his damp hair and picked up another green bean.

"That's the smell of fresh green beans, tomatoes, basil and some good old homemade bread," Gail said. She got up and went to the sink to wash her hands. "But now, I'm going to leave all this in your hands, Priscilla."

"And where are you going off to?" I said, surprised to see her prepare to leave.

"Some new wannabe cowboys arrived late yesterday, and we scheduled a ride in about an hour. I'll go out to the stable and get the horses ready."

"I can do that," Preston offered.

I smiled as a relieved expression took over Gail's face. She had a lot on her plate and coordinating everything was a feat.

"And I can play the guide, if you want," Preston went on.

She sat back down, letting out a big sigh of relief. "I have to admit, son. I was hoping you'd say that. These past two weeks have been busier than I've seen in a long time. I've been reluctant to hire extra hands, but I think I might have to do just that. If you two hadn't arrived when you did, I don' know how I'd be getting on."

"I'm more than happy to help out," he said. Without saying more, he turned around and headed out, got back on his horse and turned in the direction of the campground.

"I'll ask again," Gail said, looking at me with those mischievous eyes of hers. "Can I keep him?"

I laughed and got up to go rinse off my bowlful of green beans. "I can certainly understand why you would want to."

As I ran cool water over the green beans, I looked back at Gail. Seated at the table, her head was low.

"You okay?" I called back to her.

She barely raised her head. "Oh, yes. I'm fine. Just a bit of fatigue setting in. And there's still so much to do."

I drained the water off the green beans and left the bowl on the counter. "You've been up since dawn," I said as went back to her. "And you were up last night until... what? Eleven? Midnight?"

She nodded. "I have salads to prepare. I promised them a good old, thick and rich macaroni and cheese. I also promised homemade biscuits, cheesecake, doughnuts and..." she said, counting the items off on her fingers. "And what else?" She looked to the ceiling for the answer. "Darn it. I'm beginning to forget all the things that I have to do."

151

"You're overdoing it, Gail." I put my hand to her shoulder. "Why don't you go back to bed for a while and let me take care of some of those things."

"I can't do that. There's too much and you…"

"I… what?" I said, challenging her. "I can't bake? I can't cook? I can prepare a meal?"

"Oh, honey. No. That's not what I meant."

"I know how to make cheesecake and, you might not know it by looking at me, but I make a mean biscuit."

She laughed. "Oh, honey. I know that you're capable of doing just about anything you set your mind to."

"So, does that mean that you'll head off to bed for an hour or two."

She stood up, the exhaustion evident in her hooded eyes. "Okay. Just an hour. Not a minute more. Come wake me up in an hour."

"Go," I said simply.

She nodded and walked out. And I went into action. The rest of the morning was a surprisingly satisfying flurry of measuring, stirring and baking. I found it soothing to plunge my hands into the thick dough to make biscuits. My doughnuts came out better than I expected. And my cheesecake... As I placed a few decorative fresh strawberries on top, I knew that Gail would be proud to serve it to her guests.

With everything set, I grabbed Gail's laptop and headed out to the patio. I was still reluctant to use my phone for now, but I was eager to look up a few things.

I'd spent over half an hour poking around here and there when I looked up to see Preston returning from his ride with Gail's five new guests.

The men smiled and laughed their satisfaction and seemed genuinely please with Preston. I could only imagine where he'd brought them and the adventure he'd offered them.

"You were supposed to wake me up an hour ago."

Startled, I let out a yelp and turned to see Gail, sleepy-eyed, standing behind me.

"Oh," I said with mock surprise and confusion. "Has it been an hour already?"

She laughed and looked back inside the kitchen. "You've been busy."

"I had fun."

"And that fella of yours?"

I glanced out the window to see Preston helping an older gentleman down from his horse, then guiding them inside the stable. "He seems to be enjoying himself."

At least that's how it appeared. Since arriving at Gail's ranch, he was often jovial, and there was a laidback way about him that hadn't been there before.

He came back out with the guests, smiling and waving at them as they parted ways; they to the campground and he to the house.

154

"You've got that look in your eyes," Gail whispered.

I glanced back at her. "What look? I'm just taking in the gorgeous scenery."

"Well you got that half right... it certainly is gorgeous out there, but it has nothing to do with the scenery and everything to do with the stud on two legs."

I couldn't argue with her there. Sweaty, dusty and dirty, he was the perfect rugged cowboy come to life.

"Why don't you go out there and see how his day went," Gail offered. "Then head out to the campground and I'll start bringing dinner out."

"But... Gail... I want to help..."

"You've done enough, Priscilla," she said more firmly. "Now, you go out there and be with your man."

"I told you," I argued. "He's not my man." But my heart fluttered, and my body ached.

"Go."

I didn't argue. Opening the door, I smiled back at her and went out to meet Preston.

"Hungry?" I said for lack of a better opener.

"Starving," he said with a tired but satisfied smile. "Those guys just wanted to go farther and farther out... well beyond my knowledge of the surroundings." He chuckled. "We almost got lost."

Without saying anything, I guided him back in the direction of the campground. He didn't question or fuss. Just followed along... easy, carefree... peaceful.

"And what have you been doing all day?" he said.

I looked at him and wondered where to begin. "Well, you'll probably be eating a lot of what I did?"

"Sounds good."

"You don't even know what I made."

"Doesn't matter. I'm sure it'll be good."

I glanced sidelong at him. Despite everything, he was being so sweet and patient. Our stay at Gail's seemed endless and every morning I expected him to say that he'd had enough and wanted to go back home.

But he never did. He almost seemed to embrace this new life. Was it being here at Gail's? The ranch? The horses?

Or did it have anything to do with being here with me?

"And what's the other thing?"

"What do you mean?" I said, looking innocently at him.

"You have something else that you want to tell me."

How can you tell? I wanted to say.

"Your eyes arc darting everywhere as if looking for a way to tell someone bad news," he said. "I haven't known you for long, but I've picked up on a few little things."

Fair enough, but did I really want to tell him about what I'd discovered.

While out on the patio with Gail's laptop, I'd poked around to find out more about what had happened to my father.

When younger, while intrigued, I'd never really looked into his arrest.

But now… it seemed important that I find out why he was in prison.

"So?" he said with a nudge of his elbow against my arm. "Are you going to tell me or not?"

I shrugged. "I had some time to look into my father's past."

"And…?" he said. "What did you find?"

I shrugged again. The media seemed to have had little interest in my father's case.

"I just found something regarding a scandal with Pinkerton Security," I said after a moment's hesitation.

"Pinkerton Security?" he said. "Do you mean *the* Pinkerton Security? As in the world famous Pinkertons? As in America's foremost security company?"

"That's the one," I said. I wasn't sure how much I wanted to share with him. Partly because the information that I'd found had been so sparse and, at times, vague, but also because I felt a shroud of guilt envelope me as I thought about it.

I'd always looked up to my father… strong, honest, hard-working. The thought of him committing a crime… it just seemed impossible. It wasn't in his nature.

"Go on," he said. "Don't leave me hanging."

"He was found guilty of embezzling his client's money. This was all while he was in charge of his client's security for all their companies."

"Do you know who?" he said. "What company?"

"A company called Gaslight Inc."

As we neared the campground, he stopped walking and turned to face me. "The name rings a bell," he said. "Do you know who owns it?"

"The company was bought out a few years ago."

"By who?"

"A holding company." I looked at him, still reluctant to go any further.

"After all we've been through, Priscilla, I think you owe it to me to tell me all that you know… because, somehow, for some reason, I'm starting to get the feeling that this all ties in together."

I continued to look at him.

"Am I wrong?"

I shook my head.

"Who owns this holding company? My father?"

I shook my head more vehemently.

"The company's name is Penelope Trust."

He frowned and I could see he was looking for a connection. "And…?"

"The name apparently comes from an heiress… Penelope Packard."

His eyes shot wide open. "Packard?"

I nodded. "Do you know her?"

"My mother's maiden name was Packard."

"Oh," I said with interest. I'd never stopped to consider that his uncle was on his mother's side.

"She once told me of her family's wealth. But when her father found out that she was to marry a Prickly, he was furious. He hated Jackson. Clearly he saw in Jackson what my mother refused to see. Anyway, he ended up telling her to choose. Prickly or her inheritance."

"And she chose Prickly?" I said, a little surprised.

He shrugged. "What can I say? I guess the old buzzard can be charming when he wants. No doubt, if he thought he could get to my mother's money, he'd do anything. He probably sweet talked her until he found out that she'd been cut from the will." He shrugged. "I don't know, really. All I know is that he left us not long after I was born. As you can imagine, my mother was devastated... kind of lost, actually."

"And that's why she sent you to go live with your uncle," I said.

He nodded. "My uncle did a great job of raising me… if I do say so myself."

"So, so," I said with a teasing grin as I held my palm flat out and rocked it back and forth.

Chuckling, he looked at me. "Well, he did… and all while keeping me well hidden from that monster."

"You were lucky to have him."

"Damn right, I was."

"And what did your mother do? Did she reconnect with your father?"

He shook his head. "She moved on. She'd met this guy. I never met him, but my uncle told me that he was a good guy. You know, hard working, honest, loving. All that. They were engaged and set to get married."

"And…?"

"About three weeks before the wedding, she was found dead in her apartment."

I gasped. "What happened?"

He shrugged and looked around as if wanting to shrug off the uncomfortable emotions associated with the memory of his mother.

"I'm sorry," I said. "I don't want to pry… but…"

He shrugged again. "I still don't know what really happened. My uncle refused to talk about it. But…"

"But, what?"

He shook his head and, with his hands on his hips he turned away. Raking his fingers through his hair, he turned back to me. "I have no fucking idea what happened to her. But I know that my fucking father had something to do with it. I have no proof. I have no evidence, but shit. I know he's responsible."

I wanted to reach out to take his hand. I wanted to run my fingers through his hair. I wanted to hold him, to erase the pain caused by his father.

But I just stood there, looking at him. There was so much more that I wanted to tell him. I glanced back at the campground. Everyone was waiting for the cookout. Gail would be coming out any minute now, loaded with food.

My appetite was non-existent. And if I told Preston the rest of what I'd discovered, he'd lose his appetite as well.

"I know you're holding out, Priscilla," he said looking at me from under his brow. "I'm a big boy. I can take whatever it is that you have to say."

Nodding, I guided him to a nearby bench and pulled him down to sit with me.

"That bad, huh?" he said.

"From what I could find, a while back… several years ago, Penelope Trust changed hands, as it were."

"Oh?"

"It was put in your name."

He frowned. "My name? Are you sure?"

"So, I'm guessing that you weren't aware of that."

He shook his head.

164

"For years it's been Jackson Prickly who has managed it. Seems like he sighed control of everything over to himself. He had Pinkerton Security used as the Trust's security company."

Preston leaned back and tilted his head up, looking at the sky.

"I still need to find out more," I went on. "I need to find out where my father is and find out what really happened. There's clearly a connection between the Pinkertons and the Packards... and Prickly."

Chapter 13

<u>Tip</u>

The trip to Texas was hell. The heat was stifling, even more so than in Vegas. But I finally made it to San Angelo.

I was expecting a shit town, but the place surprised me. Not only was it a quaint and welcoming town, but the people were open and friendly.

When I stopped at a gas station to fill up, I went inside to pay.

"Do you happen to know where the Packard Ranch is?" I asked the attendant, not really expecting a good answer.

"Oh, sure," she said with a smile as she pointed back where I'd come from. "You just turn back around that way, hang a left, drive out a few miles and you can't miss it."

I thanked her and headed out, eager to finally see this ranch. With Preston gone, who would be running it? And what did they know?

I followed the directions I'd been given and pulled up in front of the ranch. Impressive. Very impressive. The kid sure knew what he was doing. Everything was tidy, well-kept and appealing. The buildings all looked new, well made and probably expensive. In the distance I could see a few sheep frolicking about, but what really caught my eye were the two pick-up trucks parked near the main house.

Turning up the drive, I prepared my speech. As I pulled up behind one of the pick-up trucks, a big beef of a guy came out of the main house. Seconds later another guy came out of the barn and headed my way.

167

"What can I help you with this morning?" the big beefy guy said.

"Are you Preston?" I said, knowing full well that it wasn't him.

He shook his head. "The name is Bacon. I'm taking over for a spell." He looked up as the other guy joined us. "That's Rick."

"Nice to meet you fellas," I said, as jovial as can be.

"So," Bacon said. "What brings you out to the Packard Ranch?"

"Sheep," I said. "I've been hearing a lot of good things about this place through the grapevine. Best sheep. Special sheep."

I didn't know a fucking thing about sheep.

"That's right," Rick said. "And we take good care of them. You looking to buy wool, or what?"

I shook my head. "Sheep," I said again. "I'm thinking of starting my own ranch."

"Here in Texas?" Bacon said.

"Nope," I said. "Out in Nevada."

"Nevada?" he said, his brow creasing.

"Mind if I have a look around?" I said, wanting to avoid too many questions from him.

They looked at each other, then the big guy nodded.

"Sure," he said, waving me over to follow him. "I'll show you the place."

It was hard not to be impressed with the professional look of the place. Everything was surprisingly clean… immaculate even.

"In addition to the sheep, we have a few other farm animals," Bacon said as he pointed to the barn and the fenced in enclosure on the far side of it.

"You boys must be pretty busy," I said.

"Good honest work," he said. He pointed to another building. "We do some shearing there. The boss man likes to give the occasional on-site buyer a real feel for the product."

"I hear you have a prize sheep," I said. "Like a real… you know… stud animal or something."

"Oh," Bacon said with a chuckle. "You must be talking about Thunder. Yeah. He's a special animal, all right. And he didn't get that name by accident. When that beast bleats, it thunders throughout."

He brought me over to a stable that housed a few of the more important sheep.

"That's him over there," Bacon said. "Isn't he a beauty."

I had no idea how to tell a good sheep from a bad sheep from a special sheep from a stud sheep. The animal looked like an oversized marshmallow with a black face.

"Is this fella for sale?" I said.

He shrugged. "I guess everything's for sale if the price is right. But this big guy is worth the big money. How much were you hoping to spend?"

I had no clue what an animal like that could be worth. Instead of answering, I shrugged, and I pulled out my phone. "Mind if I take a few pictures." I held my phone up to him and waved it back and forth. "Show the wifey back home."

"Sure," he said. "Go ahead."

I got in close to the animal and even reached out to pet it all while taking another photo that included my hand in the frame. I then backed up to take a photo of the stable and farther back to take in the exterior of the building.

"That ought to do the trick," I said.

"Would you like to sample some of our wool?" Bacon said. "We have a bundle over there that we're getting ready to ship out to a potential new client."

"No need," I said, quickly turning to head back toward my car.

"Is there some way to contact you? Maybe you would like to talk to Preston personally. He should be back in a few days or so."

With a determined step, I marched on, eager to get to my car. "That won't be necessary," I called over my shoulder.

"Well, can I have your name so that I can tell Preston about…"

"Not necessary!" I shouted as I reached my car and got in.

I turned the car around and got out of there. I drove a mile or two and pulled over.

"Let's see what you have to say about this, my lovely Priscilla," I muttered as I pulled out my phone and looked at the photos I'd taken. Perfect. They were perfect.

I selected the photos and sent them to Priscilla. After waiting a few seconds for those images to sink into her brain, I wrote her a nice little message:

Was just out here in grand old San Angelo and stopped in to see how your boyfriend's sheep farm is doing.

Baa Baa

I sent the message and waited a few seconds. Then:

Prick*ly Promise (Prickly Proposal #2)

Maybe Little Boo Peep shouldn't leave her sheep alone.

There are big bad wolves everywhere.

Something is bound to happen.

Take care, love

I stayed there on the side of the road and waited. I could just imagine her face as she looked at those photos and read my little messages.

One minute. Two minutes. Three minutes and...

Ring-a-ling, ling.

"Y'hello," I chanted into the phone.

"Tip," she said, her voice tense, almost shrill.

"Priscilla, love! How nice to finally hear from you."

"Tip, if you harm those sheep..."

"Yes?" I chanted. "What will happen, Priscilla? What are you going to do if I make lamb chops out of one of those lovely little babies?"

"Don't," she said. "Don't you dare."

"Or else?"

"Tip," she said, clearly alarmed.

"You know what you have to do, Priscilla," I said, no longer playing the game. "You owe me."

"And you deceived me."

"Pay up, Priscilla. Hand over Preston and I'll never bring up the Prickly name again."

"I can't do that."

"Then, you let that boyfriend of yours know that he'll return to his little hobby ranch to find a massive slaughter."

"You wouldn't," she hissed. "I know you, Tip. You'd never do such a thing."

"Desperate times call for desperate measures, Priscilla. You've backed me up against the wall and there are no other options. I am willing to do anything that it takes to get that bounty."

"Fuck you."

"Tsk. Tsk." I looked at my phone. We'd been on the line for nearly five minutes. More than enough time to locate the source of the call. "That boy of yours is making you lose your touch,

Priscilla. You've grown soft... unprofessional. Bring him to me and we'll settle this."

"Fuck you!"

And she hung up.

"Well, little girl," I said into the dead phone. "I'm really disappointed. I thought I'd trained you better than that. Never use your phone if you don't want to be found. Your hotheadedness just cost you a bundle, my girl. A big bundle."

Chapter 14

Preston

As I got into the shower, I repeated in my head for the hundredth time the conversation I'd had with Priscilla. Her father. My father. My uncle. All tangled. All related somehow.

And it was Tip who had, in his own special way, brought Priscilla and I together.

Was that a part of Tip's plan? To unite the children whose lives Prickly had ruined?

It was impossible to know… or to know why.

My father had put my name as head of Penelope Trust. What a surprise. Was there anything he wouldn't do to get ahead, to steal, to cheat… anything to get richer?

Prick*ly Promise (Prickly Proposal #2)

Who had he defrauded and scammed all these years... potentially ruining my good name?

And for what?

I let the water run down my shoulders, over my back and down to the drain as if willing all the sins of my father to be washed away. But they didn't... and they never would. I would forever be that bastard's son. There was no getting away from it.

Shit!

I slammed my open palm against the tiled shower wall and leaned my forehead over my hand. Tears stung my eyes, but I refused to let them fall. I refused to shed a single tear because of that man.

I'd already shed far too many.

I shut off the water and toweled off then threw on a pair of boxers before taking the three steps that brought me into the kitchen. I opened the refrigerator door only to realize that I had no appetite.

The very thought of Jackson Prickly was enough to ruin anyone's appetite.

Determined to ignore the recurring pain that always accompanied any thought of him, I opened the refrigerator door again and pulled out cheese, ham and mayonnaise.

"Oh, there you are," Priscilla said as she walked in.

She was a ray of sunshine. With her hair pulled back and her cheeks reddened by the sun, she was an angel in blue jeans. And damn, those jeans fit her well. Adding to the angelic aura, she wore a thin, white cotton shirt. Dangling from the neckline were two long cords with tiny tassels at the end, and the shoulders was embroidered with small white on white flowers.

She was more of a cowgirl than I would have imagined.

The thought made me smile until I noticed the crease of her brow. "What's up?" I said, trying to keep it light.

She shrugged as she walked into the kitchen area, opened the fridge and poured herself a glass of ice cold water that I'd sliced lemon and lime into. Glancing at me over her glass, her eyes were big with worry, but she slowly sipped the ice water as if stalling.

Finally, the glass was empty, and she had to put it down.

"How come you're having lunch here?" she said, looking at the ham and cheese. "Why don't you eat at the main house."

I shrugged. "No reason." I looked pointedly at her. "So? What's up?"

Still, she stalled. She ran her hand over the drops of water that'd fallen on the counter as she'd poured the water.

"Are you going to keep me waiting for long?" I said, growing more anxious with every passing moment.

She shook her head, her eyes red with unshed tears.

Steel yourself, man. This is going to be bad.
"Tip," she said.

I nodded. "Okay."

"He went to San Angelo."

Oh, fuck. My heart skipped a beat.

"He went to Packard Ranch."

Motherfucking shit. Nausea crept into my belly.

"I don't know what..." She stopped herself and leaned back against the counter.

"No matter what he did or is planning to do," I said, fighting hard to maintain control of my emotions. "One thing is for certain... it's not good."

"He took a picture of your sheep," she said with difficulty.

I almost gagged. "He... He what?" I said, not sure I'd heard her correctly.

"Your prize sheep," she said, the words barely audible.

"Thunder?"

She nodded.

Biting my bottom lip, I shook my head. The bastard. Be it Tip who'd taken the initiative or Jackson who'd given the order... bastards all.

"I'm so sorry, Preston," Priscilla said as she gripped the edge of the counter with both hands.

Her face grew pale and for a moment, I feared she'd faint.

"This whole thing is just so crazy," she said. "Tip... I never would have thought that he'd... Shit. I don't know what to think anymore. I don't know who to trust anymore. I can't believe how he pulled the wool over my eyes."

I chuckled at the wool reference. "Considering the line of work I'm in, you'd think that I'd be the one pulling the wool over people's eyes."

She looked up at me and let out a sour snort. "I can't believe how you can find a way to laugh at a time like this," she said.

"I've had a lifetime of crying over the things that my father has done. I'm all cried out, and I'm ready to fight. And if a chuckle here and there gets me through it, then so be it."

She nodded. "I agree... but... shit." Her shoulders sagged and she hung her head low. "Shit!"

I put my hand to her shoulder and squeezed lightly. "I think you've done enough to protect me, Priscilla."

She looked up at me and her gaze instantly hardened. "And I will continue to protect you. That's my job."

"No," I said firmly. "You've been played. They used you like a pawn. Enough is enough. They dragged you into this way too deep. Way too deep. I've been shying away from my father all these years, and now he's prepared to destroy everyone in his path to get to me. Well..."

"No," she shot out. Panic filled her as she left the counter and walked around the dining table only to return and lean against the counter once again. Her breathing was jagged and hard. "No."

I looked at her, so fierce and determined. So strong and independent. But no matter how strong she was, it was time that I stood up and grabbed the bull by the horns.

If it was true that my father was responsible for Pinkerton going to jail... what would Jackson do to Pinkerton's daughter if he found out that she was investigating the whole sordid story?

Nothing good. That, I knew with certainty.

Looking at her, suddenly so vulnerable and unsure, I knew I had to do everything that I could to protect her. She didn't deserve any of this.

We stood in silence for a long moment, thinking, fearing, planning, dreading.

Her breathing finally returned to normal, and she straightened up slightly. "I know Tip," she said softly. "I don't think that he would really hurt your animals."

I glanced sidelong at her. "My father can be a very persuasive man. Believe me. He's pushed men to do far worse than kill a sheep."

She shivered and hugged herself. "Still..." she murmured to herself. "He's been like a father to me these last years. I can't believe that he could do something so horrible... that he could do anything that could hurt me in any way... in any way."

"Look," I said with a smirk. "Don't worry about my sheep. You've met Bacon and Rick. Do they look like that type of guys who would let someone like Tip even get close to my sheep?"

"Well, Tip did get close enough to take a photo."

I looked at her. She had a point.

"Can I see the photo?"

She nodded and pulled her phone from out of her back pocket. She found the photo and showed me the screen.

184

It was Thunder, all right. And there in the frame of one of the photos was Tip's fucking, pudgy little hand.

Fuck!

"Okay," I said, swallowing my anger. "I'll get in touch with the guys right away and tell them to be more vigilant. I'll tell them to keep all other ranch hands close by."

We both turned to the door as Gail called out Priscilla's name.

"I hate to leave you alone to deal with that awful bit of news."

"Go," I said. "Gail needs you. Considering everything that she's doing for us, the least we can do is help her out any way we can."

Still, she looked at me, hesitantly. "I think that, under the circumstances, she'd understand if I didn't..."

"No. Whether she understands or not is beside the point. Go."

"But..."

"Go, Priscilla. We'll discuss this later."

She looked at me for a long, hard moment, but didn't argue. She came to me, kissed me on the cheek and left.

I went to the door and watched her take the path that led to the back of the main house. Her stride was quick and nervous while her hands fidgeted from the stress of it all.

Shit. Everything was getting worse by the minute.

I turned away and pulled out my phone. "Bacon," I barked when he answered. "What's going on?"

"Hey, Pres. Good to hear from you, man. Everything is running smoothly out here. We had Ms. Torn come by yesterday to check out that sample bundle of wool, and today Mr. Carlos is set to come. I'm sure he'll put in a big purchase. How about you? Did you win the jackpot in Vegas? Are you coming back soon?"

"Did you get an unexpected visitor?" I said, ignoring all his questions.

He hesitated, then said, "Uh. Yeah. How'd you know?"

"What'd he want?"

"Something about starting a sheep farm out in..." He grunted. "Oh, shit. He was from Nevada."

"An older guy? Big. Slightly balding."

"Yeah. That's the one."

"Listen carefully, Bacon. I want everyone, and I mean everyone on high alert. Look at this guy's visit as a literal attack. My ranch is being attacked and I want you guys vigilant and looking out for every tiny little thing. Cancel all visits to the ranch."

"Even Mr. Carlos."

"All of them."

"Sure. Look, man. Don't freak out too much."

"How can I not freak out?"

187

"Listen," Bacon said. "Maybe the guy fooled me when he first arrived, but... The guy was smooth, but his story was a little strange. It didn't add up. And the way he just ran off. Weird. So I warned the guys to be on the look-out for trouble."

"Beef up security, Bacon."

"Rick is out there right now with Luis setting up new security cameras."

"Good. And see if you can't hire a few more guys to help out. I know that the Granger Ranch recently let three of their guys go. Good men. Duncan, Pete and..." I searched for the name. "Keith."

"Yeah," he said. "I know them. Hard workers."

"See if you can't sign them up."

"Sure thing. And, hey man, I kind of spread the word to other ranches around here. I let them know that something fishy is going on and to keep their eyes and ears open."

"Good. That's good." Nodding, I stared out the window, looking at Gail as she struggled to drag a picnic table across the patio. "That's good, Bacon," I muttered softly. "You guys take care."

"Sure thing, boss."

"Let me know the minute something comes up."

"Will do."

I ended the call feeling somewhat relieved. Bacon and Rick were two of the most hard-working and resourceful guys in the business. I knew I could count on them.

But I also knew that they were up against something big.

As I shoved my phone into my back pocket, I headed out. In the distance, Gail was carrying a large flowerpot, struggling with the weight and size of the thing.

Why wasn't Priscilla there to help her?

"Need a hand?" I said as I came up to her.

"Oh, Preston," she said. "Yes. I have three of these things that I want to set up there along the perimeter of the patio."

I picked up one of the large flowerpots and carried it to the edge of the patio. "Where's Priscilla?"

"I don't know."

I set the pot down with a bit more of a clatter than planned and quickly straightened up to look at Gail. "What do you mean you don't know? Didn't she come out here to help you?"

She shrugged. "I called her." She shrugged again. "When she didn't come, I figured she was busy with something else."

I looked around.

Gail came up to me and put her hand to my shoulder. "I have a million and one things going on in the kitchen. A new band of cowboys just set up in my Galveston cabin and that honeymoon couple in the Phoenix cabin is going to want something special… a nice newlywed cake. I really need to get back inside."

I nodded as I scanned the surroundings. "Sure," I muttered. "I'll find Priscilla and send her over to help you out."

Heading to the gardens, my heart pounded uncomfortably. There was no way that Priscilla would ignore Gail's call for help. Maybe she'd seen one of the dogs in trouble and run off to help it. But where?

I turned and walked to the stables. Maybe she'd heard a disturbance and had come out to see what the problem was.

"Hey, guys," I called out to the horses that all looked up at me as I walked in. I made a beeline for Ralph. "Have you seen Priscilla."

With a snort, he shook his head then leaned over the gate for a treat.

"Sorry," I said, holding my empty hands up to him. "I have nothing for you today."

I headed out. With my hands on my hips, I looked around, confused.

No way she would just stroll out into the desert for the hell of it.

"Where the hell did you go?" I called out gently. I looked around at the immensity of the property. "Priscilla!"

Dead air.

"Priscilla!"

As I continued to walk the grounds, I pulled out my phone and called her. "Answer, Priscilla. Answer."

After five rings, an answer.

"Hello…"

"Priscilla, where are you?"

"You've reached Priscilla Pinkerton. I'm unable to take your call at the moment but if you leave a message, I'll get back to you shortly."

Shit. Her voicemail.

"Where are you?" It was the simple and short message that I left hoping she'd call back.

But I didn't hold my breath.

I headed down the long drive that led to the main road and called her once again. In the distance, I heard the faint sound of Priscilla's favorite Elvis song… *Such a Night*… her ringtone.

My heart pounded so hard, I thought I'd have a heart attack right then and there. No fucking way was it a good thing to be hearing her Elvis song out here with her nowhere in sight.

Before I could find the phone, the voicemail came on again. I hung up and called again, this time with my ear cued to hear Elvis and not the ringing in my own phone.

I got closer and closer to the sounds of the song. It got louder and louder. And there it was, lying in the tall sawgrass that grew along the edge of the driveway.

"What the fuck!" I let out. "What the fucking fuck?"

Panic took over me. My breathing was jagged and painful, and the aching in my chest grew unbearable.

Please, I called to the heavens. No! Tell me that she just ran out here to get the mail and she dropped her phone. Tell me that she ran out here to greet a delivery man and she dropped her phone. Tell me that she ran out here to catch one of Gail's dogs, and she dropped her phone.

Fuck! Just tell me that she dropped her phone!

Tears stung my eyes with the realization that it was none of that.

Her phone was hidden in a bush besides the road, and Priscilla was gone.

Chapter 15

<u>Priscilla</u>

It had all happened so quickly.

It'd been the perfect day. Hot, but pleasant. Bright sunlight. Birds singing. Such a beautiful day. The dogs had been scampering around. Guests were setting up in the campground. In the distance Gail had returned inside for a moment after calling for me.

A white van pulled into the drive. A young couple. They seemed lost. Hesitant. A woman got out and, with the flat of her hand shielding her eyes from the sun, she looked up at the house, confused.

Instead of heading straight to the house, I turned to help the lost tourists.

They were very young. A good-looking couple. Smiling. Happy.

"I'm so sorry to disturb you?" the young woman said. "But, is this Gail's Dude Ranch?"

"Yes," I said. "That's right. You can just drive right up to the house and…"

"Are you Gail?"

"No," I said. "I'm just here to help out." I extended my hand out to her. "I'm Priscilla."

"Oh," she said with a friendly smile. "What a pretty name."

"Hey," the guy called from inside the white van. "Do you know where the closest burger joint is?"

Smiling and happy to help, I came up to the passenger door window. "We've got great food right here. If you want, I can go in with you and get you set up."

As I spoke, I noticed the strange and discomforting grin on the man's face, and as the girl came right up behind me, a chill ran up the back of

196

my neck. I glanced sidelong into the back of the van. It wasn't an RV van set up to camp in. No. The back space was littered with weapons, rope and tie-wraps.

"Get in," the girl said as she pressed closer to me.

"Wait. What?" I said, momentarily confused. But I understood fast enough.

They weren't tourists at all.

The man behind the wheel stood and came to the sliding door on the side of the van and the girl shoved me inside.

Before I knew what was happening, a black fabric sac was thrown over my head turning everything dark. The drawstring was pulled tight, just barely leaving me room to breathe.

"Get us out of here," the girl ordered as she yanked my arms behind my back and gathered my wrists together.

The van lurched forward almost tossing us both back as the girl grabbed a nylon cable tie and slipped the already formed loop around both my wrists.

I consciously clasped my hands together in a way that kept my wrists as far apart as necessary. The girl didn't notice and pulled the nylon tie tight and – to her thinking – secure. But I had just enough of a wiggle room.

"Sit tight," she said as she left me. "It's a short ride."

The driver made a quick left turn that sent me falling back and I hit my head against the wall of the van.

Everything went blacker than black.

Now, as the bumpy ride shook me out of my unconscious state, I sat back and leaned against the wall of the van. In the distance, the sound of voices came to me.

The same couple that'd come up the drive?

Or someone new?

I couldn't tell. All I knew is that I was now the bounty to hunters who'd been sent to capture me. People like me who worked for a living, finding people and bringing them back.

Only I had never tied anyone up and thrown them in the back of a van.

Straining to hear what was being said, I leaned forward but was still unable to understand anything. I inched closer to the sound of the voices.

"...I told you we'd be the first to find her," the man was saying. "Priscilla, fucking Pinkerton, right here in our fucking truck." He snapped his fingers. "Easy like that. Told you. I fucking told you we could do this."

"Right," the girl said. "All we have to do now to collect that six-figure bounty is get her to that Prickly guy alive."

They were bringing me to Jackson. I shuddered at the thought. But Tip had mentioned the possibility. Had I ignored it? Had I been so wrapped up with my seemingly peaceful days at the ranch that I didn't take him seriously enough?

Shit.

All of my training, all of my years of experience seemed to be dripping off my fingertips and flowing away and there was nothing I could do about it.

Preston? Was he the reason I was growing… what? Soft? Distracted? Unprofessional?

Well, I would have to remedy that quickly enough.

I shifted back to the far end of the van. With my wrist so loosely bound, I freed my hands then slowly and carefully tried to pull the black sac off my head. The damned thing was knotted at the back… a good, stiff knot.

Pulling a small pocket knife out of my boot, I flicked it open and reached up to cut the cord that held the sac securely over my head.

Fully freed of all constraints, all that remained was finding a way out of the van without my captors noticing. I glanced outside the window…. desert. Miles and miles of desert.

I knew that Jackson's building was in the heart of Vegas. At least that was where I'd been instructed to bring Preston. Was that where they were bringing me?

Judging by the view outside the window we were somewhere between Gail's ranch and Vegas.

Now what?

Get out.

Right. But how?

I looked around. The sliding door behind the passenger seat was out of the question. The girl would not only hear me open the door, but she and her driver would surely see me in the side door mirror.

The back doors?

What were the chances that the driver would see me open the back door in his rearview mirror? The chances were high. Very high. The minute I opened the door the sun's rays would pour in. It would be impossible to miss.

So?

Think. Think Pinkerton. Think.
The windows?
No.

Then, as the couple burst out laughing, I looked at the front of the van and noticed that there wasn't a rearview mirror at all.

Yes!

I inched my way to the back door and grabbed the door handle. It would be easy enough to open. I glanced at my captors as their voices suddenly grew louder.

"… and I think that we should buy a house!" the woman shouted.

"What the fuck for?" the man shouted back. "We have an apartment. We have a great apartment."

"We fucking live in your mother's living room, and it's not that great of an apartment. I want my own place!"

"And I want to use the money to get a real car… a sports car. Something snazzy that I can drive up the Strip with."

"What for? To attract babes?"

"No. You're my babe."

"Well, it won't be a car. We're not going to do that. I want a house. Something out in Henderson."

"Henderson?" he said. "When the fuck did you get so uppity?"

"Henderson is not uppity," she shouted back. "It's a beautiful neighborhood."

Taking advantage of their shouting match over how to spend their bounty money, I slowly pulled down on the handle to the back door. Immediately I felt a rush of air as I tried to pull the door completely open. But I hung on, keeping it just barely ajar.

"I knew you'd be an idiot about this," the girl screamed. "Can't you just for once give me what I want? Can't you just let me have my way this one time? Fuck! You're such an insensitive bastard when you want."

As she ranted on, I opened the door and, grabbing the outside handle on the other door, I squeezed through the narrow opening. Standing on the back bumper, I struggled to keep my balance.

"You're the idiot about all this," I heard the guy shout as I slowly and gently closed the door until the locking mechanism rested up against the other door. "Shit, you're an idiot!"

I managed to clamp the door shut. Walking to the right side of the van, I peeked around the front. We were arriving at a sharp bend to the left. *Perfect.*

We approached. Closer. My entire body was on high alert. Get ready. Not now… not now…

Now!

I jumped off the bumper just as the van veered to the left leaving me to fall in the loose desert sand. I quickly rolled away from the road and lay behind a series of creosote bushes until the van completely disappeared.

Convinced they were far enough; I stood and dusted the sand off of me.

"Great," I thought as I looked around to get my bearings. "Now what?"

Charleston Peak was to my left. In the distance I could just barely make out the silhouette of the taller buildings along the Strip.

I was about midway between the ranch and any visible sign of life. No houses. No barns. No buildings.

Okay…

How long before that pair of idiots realize I'm gone?

Could be hours. Could be minutes.

Phone. I have to get to a phone.

Going back to the ranch would be futile. My cover was blown and there was a good chance that they would head back there to find me once again.

So, forward it is.

Prick*ly Promise (Prickly Proposal #2)

I walked, then jogged, then ran a good part of
the way until I came to a rise and finally saw
buildings up ahead. Slowing down to a jog and
finally a tired walk, I made my way to the first
house.

While there was no visible sign of anyone
outside, there was a car parked in the drive.

Good sign.

I walked up the path to the front porch.

"Please, let someone be home," I muttered.
"Please let them have a phone."

All that mattered now was calling Preston to
warn him about these new bounty hunters that were
after us. He was compromised. We were all
compromised.

He had to get out of there before they reached
him.

Chapter 16

Priscilla

I was sweaty. I was dirty. I was stinky. I'd been walking, jogging and running my way back to civilization and now I was a mess.

Seeing my reflection in the window of the front door, I hesitated. If anyone was in fact at this house, would they let me in looking like this?

I looked around. The house was well-kept, the yard clean and tidy, and all along the perimeter of the front porch, flowerpots were set up with dazzling and bright colored blooms.

Running my hands through my hair, I tried to tidy up, but it was no use. I was a mess no matter what I did.

Bite the bullet and knock. Preston is counting on you.

Right.

I knocked.

"Coming," a woman called from the depths of the small house.

It seemed like an interminable amount of time passed before the door finally creaked open.

"Oh, my Lord" the woman gasped. "Bless you, child. You must be on the verge of a heatstroke. Look at those red cheeks. Come in. Come in from that infernal sun and cool off."

Though tall and heavy set, she was old and seemed a little frail. As she backed up to fully open the door, she limped slightly, her shoulders hunched forward.

"I'm so sorry to bother you, ma'am," I said, quickly feeling guilty for forcing the lame woman to her feet.

The woman waved my concern away and hobbled another step back, welcoming me in. "Come. Come. I'll bring you a cool washcloth."

"Thank you," I said as I followed her inside. "But, actually, I would really appreciate the use of your phone."

"Oh," the woman said with a pleasant smile. "Certainly. Why not do both." She gestured to her elegant but old-fashioned sofa.

"Thank you."

"What on earth has you walking out and about in this weather?" the woman called back as she headed to the kitchen. "Heat like this can be deadly. And on the side of the road... with no shade..."

"Yes. It is pretty intense."

"I was just brewing up some tea," the woman called out. "So nice. So soothing. Despite the heat, I do enjoy a nice cup of tea."

I looked around for a phone. That was my main mission, my main objective. I'd thought for certain the older woman would have a landline. I looked and looked but there was no sign of a phone.

But then I spotted the few photos set up in silver frames on the end table. My heart skipped a beat.

Okay. Calm down. It doesn't mean anything.

One photo was of a boy, perhaps ten or eleven years old, holding a soccer ball. Another showed a lovely and loving couple; their wedding photo. And finally a photo of the couple, the boy and a beautiful baby.

The only problem; all the photos were of African Americans. The old woman who'd opened the door for me was lily white.

Could it be her family?

Possibly.

Could she have adopted the man or woman in the photos?

Yes.

210

I was willing to accept that explanation until I spotted another photo from the wedding. This one showed the parents of both the bride and the groom on either side of the couple.

The old woman returned with two elegant cups of tea.

"Thank you," I said as I accepted the cup that she handed me, noting that she hadn't brought the cool washcloth as had been offered. While it would have been nice, I didn't bring it up. "I was looking for your phone… and I noticed all these photos."

A little startled and surprised, she looked at the photos that I pointed to. "Oh?"

"Is this your family?"

"Aren't they beautiful," she said with a strange smile as she sat in the chair across from me.

"Are any of them home?"

"Your tea will get cold," she said, gesturing with her hand that I drink up.

I brought the cup up to my lips. Steam rose from the hot liquid, and I gently blew over the surface of the tea, then took a discreet whiff.

Strange.

"What sort of tea is this?" I said, taking another whiff. "It smells... sort of..." I took yet another sniff.

Medicinal? That's what it smelled like. Chemical. Unnatural. Pharmaceutical.

"It's a blend of chamomile and mint," the older woman said. "My own special blend. The mint gives it that odd but satisfying kick."

No, I thought. The tea smelled nothing like mint and everything like a drug. Something strong... a sedative.

Shit. How could this be?

"And about your phone?" I said as I glanced at the front door, ready to bolt at any moment. "I really do need to make that call."

"I'll go get it," she said. "Enjoy your tea and I'll bring it right out."

She stood and looked pointedly at me. "In my day, a refusal to drink someone's special blend of tea would have been seen as the highest insult. I work so hard on that blend... so hard."

This was getting me nowhere. I set the teacup down on the side table and stood.

"Sit down," the woman said, her voice half frail and old, half solid and almost manly.

"I'm sorry?" I said, not sure I'd understood correctly.

The old woman jacked up her skirt exposing stocky, hairy legs. She reached for the gun in the holster that was strapped to her thigh.

"You heard me." There was no longer any sign of the feminine charade in her voice. She... *he* had dropped it entirely. "Sit the fuck down."

Holding the gun up at me, he removed the curly white wig and tossed it onto the armchair.

With my eyes glued to his, I sat back down. "Can you please explain what... why...?"

"Your face has been plastered on my laptop all morning. Six figure compensation for bringing your sweet little face in to one very rich Mr. Prickly. Yep. And imagine my luck when I saw you walking up that path. Angels must surely be looking down on me today to have brought you to me."

"I think you have me mixed up with…"

"Pinkerton," he said. "Priscilla Pinkerton. I would know that sweet face anywhere. No amount of dirt and grime is gonna change that."

He reached back into a cabinet and pulled out a phone. "Just gotta call Mr. Prickly himself and tell him that I have what he wants." He chuckled to himself. "Maybe I'll even have him increase the reward a little bit. I mean, if he wants you bad enough, he'll give anything… right?"

He winked at me, and I shuddered.

Chapter 17

Preston

With Priscilla's phone in hand, I marched back to the main house. I knew that Gail would be devastated by the news and, while I hesitated to cause any grief to the woman, I knew I had no choice.

She had to know.

I ran up to the front porch and barged in without knocking.

"Gail," I called out.

The house was strangely silent.

As I made my way toward the kitchen, I saw the tip of her shoes, her calves, her legs... she was seated at the kitchen table.

But when I entered the kitchen, she was not only seated at the table. She was tied to the chair and a napkin had been shoved into her mouth with clear white tape slapped over it.

Her eyes wide with fear, she looked up at me. "What the hell is going on?"

As I stepped forward, I glanced at the kitchen counter, laden with all the food that Gail had so busily been preparing. Then I noticed the bowl of cake batter on the floor, the wooden spoon two feet away with the content of the bowl splattered all over the floor and kitchen cabinets.

"What the hell is going on!?" I said again.

"Calm down..." a gentle female voice said from behind me.

Priscilla? No. The voice was a little too nasally.

I slowly turned around to see the young woman who'd arrived with her husband earlier that morning... Carmen and Jay. But while she'd been all smiles as she'd arrived earlier, she now looked at me with a hard gaze as she pointed her Glock at me.

"Carmen," I said. "It's me... Preston. We met this morning." I looked at the tall, gangly guy beside her. "And... Jay, right?"

"Sure," the girl said with a shrug. "Whatever."

"What's going on?" I said, even though I had a pretty good idea of what was going on. "Did you guys not appreciate your cabin? Do you want to cancel your stay? Get a reimbursement?"

"Shut up," Carmen said, waving her gun at me. "Get him, Jay."

"Wait a minute," I said as I backed away. "Hold on."

"There's no time to waste," Jay said. "We've got work to do."

"And there's no negotiating your way out of this," Carmen added.

"So, I take it you're not on your honeymoon," I said, remembering how lovey-dovey they were that morning.

"You catch on fast," Carmen said.

"Bounty hunters?" I offered.

"You're a really smart cookie, aren't you?" Carmen said. "That explains how you've managed to slip away from everyone."

She nodded at Jay. "Tie him up."

"Don't try anything funny," Jay said as he came up to me, grabbed my wrist and yanked my arm behind my back. He slipped what felt like a leather belt around my wrist then yanked my other arm back and secured it to the first.

"Be a good boy and no one will get hurt," Carmen said.

Clenching my jaw, I glanced at Gail who was absolutely shaking with fear.

"I have no intention of giving you guys any trouble," I said. "But..."

"No buts," Carmen shouted.

"Her!" I quickly said, looking down at Gail. "She has nothing to do with me. She's just the owner of this place and has no idea who I am. Let her go."

Carmen hesitated.

"You're working for my father, right?"

She shrugged.

"He's the one who offered you a reward for bringing me in, right?"

She shrugged again and clucked her tongue. "We're not in the habit of tracking people and bringing them in just for the hell of it. Yeah. A nice fat reward."

"The man who hired you is my father. If you leave Gail out of this, I can get him to give you a bigger reward. Big enough that you'll be set for life."

Carmen looked at Jay and smiled. Then she looked back at me. "Okay. Good. You get your father to double the reward."

I nodded.

219

"Besides," Carmen went on. "The bounty is for you, and you alone."

"And the Pinkerton girl," Jay added.

Carmen ignored him and smirked as she glanced at Gail. "We don't need the bitch anyway. She'll just weigh us down."

Jay grabbed my arm and, using too much unnecessary force, led me to the front door while Carmen placed a knife within reach of Gail's hands.

"I have no doubt that you're a smart and capable woman," Carmen said. "I'm sure you'll be able to get out of your predicament… and I'm sure that you're smart enough to keep your trap shut once you do succeed in freeing yourself… right?"

Gail nodded.

"Good girl." Carmen patted Gail on the head as one would a dog. "Okay!" she shouted as she joined Jay and me at the door. "What are you waiting for? Let's get this show on the road."

She gave me a hard shove in the back, sending me stumbling out the door and onto the front porch. I was about to reprimand her for the unnecessary manhandling but kept it to myself.

They led me to the car, but before shoving me into the back seat, Carmen, with dramatic flourish, removed the floral scarf from around her neck and blindfolded me with it.

"Is this really necessary?" I said with a wry chuckle.

"I don't care whether it is or not," Carmen said. "It's just the way I operate. So, shut up, be a good boy and this will all be over soon enough."

She knotted the scarf good and tight, then Jay guided me into the back seat and buckled me up.

"Well, thank you," I said, amused by the gesture.

As we drove off, I tried to keep track of every turn, but it soon became impossible as they got onto the highway, got off, then on again. They did everything they could to deliberately confuse me.

I gave up keeping track and just accepted that I was finally going to have to face my father.

Without warning, the car suddenly came to a full stop, the engine was cut, and the front car doors opened and slammed shut. Then the back door opened, and a smaller hand grabbed my arm and pulled me out.

"I can't believe that we did it," Carmen said as she guided me inside a building.

"Good thing," Jay said. "I've already spent a few grand of that bounty money."

Once inside, I could smell the newness of the building. Every footstep echoed loudly as we walked in a vast space. In the distance, the sound of a bell... an elevator?

There were no other footsteps. Just ours.

We stopped. I assumed in front of the elevator.

The bell. The sliding of the doors as they opened.

"Get in," Carmen said, pushing me inside.

We turned to face the doors. One of them pressed the desired floor and the elevator lurched up...high... higher... higher.

My knees buckled as the elevator came to a stop.

The bell. The doors opened.

"This way," Carmen said as she led me out of the elevator and pulled me to the left.

We walked down a long and quiet corridor and stopped suddenly.

A knock on the door. A moment's hesitation. The doorknob was turned, and the door opened.

The faint sound of a feminine gasp... familiar. So familiar.

"Go," Carmen said. She pushed me inside then shoved me back and I fell into a chair. With a violent yank, she pulled off my blindfold.

The room was flooded with sunlight, initially blinding me as I tried to focus on my surroundings. After a few seconds I was able to make out a large desk, a dark chair, and a subdued and elegant bar stocked with expensive tequila, whiskey and gin. Several posh leather armchairs were set along one side of the office and I was finally able to focus enough to take a good look at the person seated in one of those leather armchairs.

"Priscilla," I whispered.

Before I could say anything more, a door at the far end of the large office opened and an imposing man entered.

A chill shook me. It was like looking into a mirror… a time warp mirror.

The eyes were the same. The arch of the brow was the same. The slope of the nose, the curve of the mouth, the strength of the chin… same, same, same.

And while we both wore our hair in a similar fashion, with mine being slightly longer, his hair was gray and thinning. There was the hint of crow's feet at his eyes and a slight sagging of the skin under his otherwise strong chin.

Older, but the same.

Older, but still very handsome, appealing and even sensual.

It was no wonder my mother had fallen head over heels for him.

The big man snorted as he looked at me. "A chip off the old block, huh... Preston," Jackson Prickly said.

Chapter 18

<u>Priscilla</u>

I closed my eyes and tried to understand just how I had so completely lost control of the situation. It seemed like at every turn, my world changed and there was little I could do about it.

When the old lady had pulled off her wig and pulled out that gun... damn. I was overcome with nausea and saw no way out.

And there was no way out.

Seated in a large office, I opened my eyes and looked out the window, trying to ignore the sensation of that woman's... that man's hand on me as he'd grabbed my arm and unceremoniously threw me into the passenger seat of his old car.

"I could play the game of blindfolding you," he'd said. "I could smack you over the head to knock you out, or drug you, but I like to play it straight. So, this is the way it's going to be."

I looked at him. The calm of his voice camouflaged well the underlying danger of the man.

"You're going to sit there and shut up," he went on. "We're going to take a little ride and you're going to play the good little girl."

Petrified of what he would do if I so much as blew a hair off my brow, I'd sat still.

Now, with my nerves on edge, with the anticipation of what was to come, my fight or flight instincts were about to blow up. It was my worst nightmare come true.

When the door opened, I fully expected to finally meet Mr. Jackson Prickly. I couldn't help but gasp when a surprisingly young couple escorted Preston into the office.

It was the ultimate failure. I'd done all that I could to protect him from his father and I'd failed.

With a quick scan, I looked for any sign of injury and found none. At least there was that.

"My job is done," the young woman said as she whipped a floral scarf from around Preston's head and pushed him into one of the chairs that lined the far wall. "You can see where you are now."

Bleary-eyed, he looked around, confused and angry. When his gaze finally found me, confusion turned to fear.

"Are you okay?" he managed to croak out.

"Shut up and sit pretty," the young woman said.

"Come on," her mate said. "Let's get out of here."

"Not before I get my six-figure reward," she said.

"I'm sorry," Preston mouthed.

I pressed a wry grin. It was I who was sorry. I had no doubt in my mind that Prickly had had me captured and brought to his office simply to use me to get Preston to do… whatever it was that he wanted with him.

Then again, I thought of my father. He held my father's fate in his hands. What would he do with that power? What would he ask of me in exchange for the release of my father?

A discreet door beside the bar opened and I held my breath.

In walked a tall, well-built man that was the spitting image of Preston. It was like looking into the future.

The man was handsome; dangerously so. How many women had fallen for him at first glance, only to learn of the dark heart that resided in his cold chest?

"Well, well, well," he said, his eyes on Preston. He took a few steps closer to his son and took a good long look at him. "It's good to see you, son."

Preston visibly cringed.

"Looks like I really sired a good-looking kid, didn't I?" he said with a chuckle.

"And we brought him here," the young woman said, jutting out her chin. "Where's our money?"

Prickly didn't even look at her. "You'll get your money."

"I want it now," she said, clearly unimpressed by Prickly's imposing figure.

With a grunt, he went behind his desk, opened the bottom drawer and pulled out a large paper bag. "Now get out of here," he said as he shoved the bag into her arms.

Despite the clear order to leave, she unfurled the flap of the bag and looked inside, then smiled. "We're good," she said to her mate before turning to Prickly with her hand extended to him. "It's good doing business with you."

He sneered. "Just get out, will you?"

The couple left and the silence that followed was heavy and tense.

Prick*ly Promise (Prickly Proposal #2)

What now?

Prickly brought his attention back to Preston, then shot a comical glance at me. "He's definitely a ladies' man, isn't he? Just like the old man."

"And that's where the resemblance ends," Preston said. "Our similarities are only on the surface. Contrary to you, I have a heart. I have values. I have morals. I know the difference between right and wrong."

With a crooked smile, Prickly went behind his desk and sat down. "Oh, you think? You really think that we have nothing in common, son?"

"Don't call me that," Preston spat. "I haven't been your son since the day you walked out on us."

Prickly shook his head in dismay. "That was ages ago, son… Preston. Get over it. Life doesn't always go the way we want it to. Shit happens. Shit comes in and ruins all your plans. You have to learn to be flexible and roll with the punches."

Preston snorted.

"You're like your old man a lot more than you think," Prickly went on. "Just look at the successful operation you have going there in San..." He snapped his fingers.

"San Angelo," Preston finished for him.

"Yeah," Prickly said dismissively. "Never heard of the place, but... hey. If my son wants to make it big in a small town, that's fine by me."

"Funny," Preston said. "I don't remember requesting your approval. And Lord knows that I've never made a decision in my life that revolved around your approval. I couldn't give a shit what you think... about me, about my life, about my business."

"Like it or not, boy. You inherited my smarts. I can guarantee that it's not your mother who passed on an intelligent gene. No. She passed onto you that soft side."

Preston pursed his lips then sneered as he gripped the arms of the chair. "Don't bring her into this. You have no business discussing her at all."

"Fine. Fine," Prickly said with a wave of his hand.

"What do you want?" Preston shot out.

Jackson held his palms up as if surprised by the question. "What? I want to see my son who refuses to come visit me. Can't I have a nice visit with my own son?"

"You're the one who ran off, remember?" Jackson snorted.

"All throughout my childhood, through my teens... not a word from you. No attempt at contact at all. And now... out of the blue, you decide that it's time we meet? Well, fuck you!"

"Tsk. Tsk." Jackson shook his head.

"And after what you did to my mother. Fuck you!" He bolted out of the armchair.

"Sit down, Preston."

"Why the hell should I do anything for you? Why the hell should I allow myself to be subjected to your whim?" He put his hand to the doorknob.

"You know better than to walk out that door," Jackson said. "Do you really think that I don't have guards out there to ensure that you stay right where I want you?"

With a grimace, Preston looked at me then sat back down.

"Good boy," Jackson said. "You know… for somebody who is about to inherit a small fortune, you sure are an ungrateful little bugger, aren't you?"

Preston's eyes narrowed with suspicion and doubt.

"That's right," Jackson said. "If this young lady had made that point clear to you… and if she'd stopped running away from me…"

"Don't fucking try to blame her for your ineptitudes… father," Preston said with disgust. "Really? Sending a bounty hunter out after me? Sending your fucking goons out after me?"

"All a big misunderstanding, son," Jackson said. "Just a big misunderstanding."

"Fuck your misunderstanding," Preston spat. "My being here has nothing to do with any fucking inheritance and everything to do with you conniving to get something from me. What is it? My ranch? My blood? My life? What the fuck do you want?"

"Son...

"And what the fuck does she have to do with any of this?" Preston went on, pointing at me. "Let her go. Let her go and then you and I can have a talk... man to man."

Jackson chuckled. "How noble. I'll give you that." He turned to look at me. "My son's a real gentleman, isn't he, Missy?"

I just looked at him, expressionless.

His gaze was deceptively charming and warm, sending a chill up my spine. "But the thing is, Miss Priscilla Pinkerton's father is still in prison."

The chill up my spine turned into an electric jolt. My heart suddenly pounded from the tension and tears sprang to my eyes despite my desperate attempt to keep them in check.

"He's in prison for a really bad crime," Jackson went on. "A major crime. The way things are going, he's set to stay there for a really, really long time." He shrugged. "Probably for the rest of his miserable life."

"He's not the one who committed a crime, and you know it," I said, trying to keep control of my voice. "You're the one who set him up. You're the one who framed him. You're the one who stole from his clients. You're the one who embezzled."

"Oh," Jackson said with mock shock. "Such big, ugly words for such a beautiful young lady."

"Admit it," I said. "You're the one who sent him to prison."

"Have you been playing detective, Missy?" he said. "Browsing here and there on the internet? Picking up a few clues? You're smart enough to know that you shouldn't believe everything you read... especially on the internet."

"Nice try," I said. "But I went to reputable sites that actually tell it like it is… probably sites that are run by people who are not under your oppressive thumb."

He burst out laughing and looked at Preston while pointing at me. "I like her. I really like her."

His smile gone, he turned back to look at me again. "There's only so much any news outlet can know about this situation, and you would be better served to keep your mind open and not be so quick to jump to conclusions."

"My mind is wide open… thank you very much," I shot back at him.

"I suspect that you didn't know your father all that well, Missy. I suspect that you have no idea who your father was dealing with… who his clients were?"

I shrugged. "Of course, I didn't. I was a kid… and his business was no business of mine. But I know that my father is a good and honest man… and you're not!"

Jackson shook his head. "Such impulsive youth. You are both so quick to pass judgement. You look at a situation and only see the surface level stuff. Neither of you dug in deep enough to really see what was going on. No, you kids just read some fake story, come to your fake conclusions and doled out your fake punishment. The news outlets that hate me... hate me. And they'll say anything and everything to make me look bad."

"Really, father?" Preston droned. "You're going to try to play innocent in all this? The victim of rumors and speculation? Do you really expect me to believe that you're a saint? Don't take me for an idiot."

"I never said I was a saint, but..."

"You hired a bounty hunter to find your own son," I said, disgusted by the whole sordid story. "And when I didn't bring him in as you requested, you sent your henchmen out after him... after us. And, as if that wasn't bad enough, you had Tip go all the way out to San Angelo in order for him to get

238

just enough information that he could threaten Preston with. Claiming that you're not a saint is the understatement of the century."

His eyes narrowed, but not in the sinister fashion I would have expected. He nodded. "When I want something, I don't let anything get in my way."

"No need to tell us that," Preston scoffed.

"And what I've wanted most of all these past weeks is finding my son, having him here with me, seeing him face to face."

Preston leaned forward, his elbows on his knees. "Well, I'm here... *Pops*. What the fuck is so important that you had me gagged and hogtied and brought to you."

"Hogtied?" Jackson said with a doubting frown. "Really?"

Preston shrugged.

With a quiet harrumph, Jackson stood and went to the bar. Opening a fresh new bottle of bourbon, he glanced at Preston. "How about a drink with your old man?"

Preston's eyes narrowed as he hesitated.

"After all," Jackson went on. "You're old enough now."

Preston nodded. "Sure. Why not."

Jackson poured bourbon into a tumbler and reached out to hand it to him. Holding the bottle up to show me, he looked at me, his brow quizzically cocked.

"No, thank you," I said.

"This is the good stuff," Jackson said.

"No."

"Suit yourself." He poured himself a glass and turned to Preston, holding his glass up, inviting a toast.

Preston refused and simply swirled his drink around in the glass.

As Jackson returned to his seat behind the desk, Preston rose and sat in the chair immediately across from Jackson's desk. He fixed his father with a solemn glare.

Clearly, he was tired of the games.

"We've met," Preston said. "And we've had a drink. What more do you want?"

"Sit back, son, and listen to your father," Jackson said. "You're still a young man, and I'm sure that you think that you have your life all figured out."

Preston looked silently at his father.

"I'm an ambitious man. I've always been. I admit that. I've always wanted the good things in life; a beautiful home... or two or three, luxury cars, good food, great wine... the whole thing. And I worked hard to get the good things that life has to offer. Real hard."

Pressing his lips into a sour purse, Preston mocking clapped his hands. "Well, bravo, Pops. Bravo. What do you want? A medal? A trophy? Father of the year?"

Prick*ly Promise (Prickly Proposal #2)

"It's easy to get caught up in the race," Jackson went on, ignoring his son's remarks. "The wheeling and dealing can become addictive. The fight. The battle. The win. It's so easy to forget all the other things in life… the things that money can't buy; family, affection, loyalty."

"Did you read that off of a greeting card?" Preston said with a wry grin.

"From the mouth of babes," Jackson said as he shot me an amused glance. "It's so easy for you…you two… so young… so easy to see all the years ahead of you. Plenty of time. Time to work. Time to waste. Time to play. Time. Time. Time. It seems endless. But one day, you wake up and you realize… you don't have all that much time left. You realize that you're mortal."

While Preston still smiled sardonically at his father, his eyes softened with curiosity.

"Then mortality gives you a double whammy. Not only do you have less time in front of you by the process of aging, but you now have less time in front of you because some goddamned, motherfucking shit of a cancer is eating you alive."

The sardonic grin completely fell from Preston's face. "You? Cancer?"

Jackson nodded. "Yeah. You never really know how you'll react to that sort of news until you get it. Then it hits you... hard... fucking hard. Shit. I'm not even sixty yet. And from what the doctors have told me, I'm not going to make it to sixty either. Do you know how that fucking feels? Do you know how it feels to realize that you're no longer the man you've always been? Strong? Capable? Take on the world?"

Preston shook his head, his eyes on the father that he'd just reunited with.

"When news like that strikes, you put your priorities in order." He snorted as he looked down into his glass of bourbon. He swirled the liquid around in his glass then took a swig before slamming the heavy bottomed tumbler back onto his desk. "Fuck. That's the point when you realize that your priorities are out of whack. That deal that you wanted to close... fuck it. That building that you wanted to buy... what the fuck for? Everything that you do, everything that you want... why bother?"

He leaned onto his desk and looked at his son. "No. This is when you realize the importance of family. This is when you finally understand those ties. You want to make amends and apologize. You want to fix what you've broken. You want to reconnect with those that you've lost sight of."

"Lost sight of?" Preston said, no longer angry, but still hurt. He looked down at his hands, like a little boy lost and unsure. "You didn't lose sight of me. You left. Remember?"

"I was younger than you are now when I left your mother," Jackson said. "It's not something that I'm proud of... believe me. I was a horrible father and an even worse husband. Sometimes I look back on that brash youth and wonder who he was, what he was thinking. But I was ambitious.

244

Maybe too ambitious for my own good. I didn't realize at the time how valuable what I had was." He shook his head. "What's done is done. All I can do now is tell you how sorry I am."

Preston grunted, then shuddered, as if shaken by a sob.

Jackson looked at him, his eyes imploring him. "I want to make things right."

"I don't see how you can."

As big and strong as he was, there was a brief sign of weakness in the older man's eyes. He blinked and the weakness disappeared. "I know that it doesn't make up for all the years lost," Jackson said. "My legacy. My company. My money. It's yours. All yours."

My jaw dropped.

Really?

I looked at Preston. He was equally stunned.

"Wait a minute," I said. "Are you saying that all this time, all you really wanted was to find Preston simply to give him his inheritance?"

The older man nodded as he opened the top drawer of his desk and pulled out a glossy, black folder with a white label on it that clearly read Preston. "All you have to do, son, is sign right here, here and here," he said as he pointed to various lines on three separate pages. He pulled out a gold pen, set it atop the black folder and slid it toward Preston.

I didn't know what to believe anymore. Was this just another trap? Was he toying with Preston? How easy would it be for him to claim he was sick only to trick Preston into signing something that he shouldn't sign?

"Read it carefully," I said, despite my desire to stay out of his personal affairs.

Preston nodded then picked up the pen and set it aside, then opened the folder and picked up the documents.

It could be a trick, I wanted to add. So many warnings that I wanted to shout at him.

But Preston took his time reading the long, formal documents. While I was too far to read the document, it did appear to be legitimate… prepared by lawyers.

Poking his tongue into his cheek, Preston glanced up at Jackson with a degree of understanding that wasn't there before, then nodded. He set the document down, picked up the pen and, after a brief moment of hesitation, signed the documents.

I'd managed to hold my tongue, but now wondered if I'd regret it. I couldn't help but think that Preston had allowed himself to become too emotional.

I had to hope that I was wrong.

Getting to his feet, Preston pushed the folder across the desk to his father. "There you go."

Jackson stood and faced his son, a calm expression of relief in his eyes. He picked up the pen that Preston had used and also signed the document on the necessary lines. Closing the folder, he smiled a tired smile.

"Wise decision, son," Jackson said as he walked around his desk and stood before his son. "You'll see. This is for the best."

The two men looked at each other. Preston's face softened as he took a step forward then reached out to hug the older man.

Stunned, I watched the two men as the years of anger and misunderstanding faded away. My heart wanted the scene to play out... a bittersweet ending to a long and sad story. But my gut questioned what my eyes were seeing.

Could I have been so wrong about Jackson Prickly?

But all the crimes? The henchmen? Tip's threats? What about Penelope? What about Preston's mother?

I shook my head as the two men parted and looked at each other, the lost years completely forgotten.

I longed to see the papers that Preston had signed. What was written that had so changed his view of his father? Whatever it was, I had to trust that Preston knew what he was doing.

Seeing that the older Prickly was warm and receptive, I stood. Now was my time to ask him about my father.

But a knock at the door stopped me.

"Come in," Jackson said as he resumed his big man stance.

The door opened and a man in his mid-forties walked in, a stethoscope around his neck.

"Doctor Hesseman," Jackson said, beaming with pride. "I'd like you to meet my son, Preston."

The doctor turned to Preston. "Nice to meet you. I've heard a lot about you. Mr. Prickly talks about you all the time. Constantly, even."

Preston shook the man's hand, his brow furrowed with questions.

"I'm happy to see that you've finally reunited with your son, Jackson," the doctor said. "Does this mean that you're ready to start treatment? If you put it off any longer, I can't tell you how long you'll have left."

Preston looked at me, his eyes wide with the realization that it was all true. His father really was sick and could potentially die soon. I pressed a wan smile and nodded my understanding.

Jackson put his hand to Preston's shoulder. "Nothing is holding me back now," he said, his voice cracking somewhat. "Everything's been taken care of… and just in time, too. I can leave this good Earth with my conscious clear." He slapped his hands together. "No unfinished business."

"Good to hear," the doctor said.

Jackson Prickly turned to look at me. "And to top it all off, look at his wonderful fiancé. Now that is a woman who truly loves her man… who'd do anything to protect him and do right by him."

Shocked by his declaration and a little embarrassed by the sudden attention thrown my way, I looked at the three pairs of eyes and felt the rush of blood burn my cheeks.

"Not only do I have the assurance that she truly loves him for who he is, but I now know that the Prickly legacy will live on and will be well taken care of."

"But, Mr. Prickly…," I began, wanting to set the record straight and tell him that we weren't truly engaged to be married.

"Congratulations," Doctor Hesseman said. He shook Preston's hand then reached out to take mine.

"Well," Jackson said with finality. "Now that everything has been taken care of, I'll finally get around to following the doctor's orders." He headed for the door and looked at his doctor. "Let's go beat this thing."

The two men left, leaving Preston and I alone in the office. For a stunned moment, we stood in silence, letting it all sink in.

"What just happened?" Preston finally said with a chuckle.

Smiling, I shook my head.

"Everything turned out so much better than I could ever have expected," he said softly, still in disbelief.

"You don't say."

He looked at me with a silly, cockeyed grin. "Look at us. We're a mess."

I'd completely forgotten my disheveled appearance. What must that doctor have thought?

"How about we head back to Gail's and get cleaned up?"

I nodded.

Then what? I wondered. Do we part ways? Is this the end of the road for us? The only reason we were together at all was so that I could protect him from his father.

With that threat now extinguished…

I looked at him wondering if he was asking himself the same questions.

"We never did get around to fully taking in the Vegas experience," he said.

I smiled as my gut did a somersault.

"How about we set things straight with Gail, get all gussied up and really get to know Vegas."

"Sounds good to me," I said.

Just minutes earlier, I'd feared for my life. But the situation had done a full 180 and I was now facing a wonderful evening with the man that I...

Hmm.

Loved?

Hell, yeah, I loved him.

The only question that remained was, how did he feel about me?

"Come on," Preston said as he opened the door. "Let's finish what we'd started before we were so unexpectedly interrupted."

I leaned into him as we walked out. "So? To the Bellagio fountains?"

He nodded. "To the Bellagio fountains."

Chapter 19

Priscilla

The nightmare was over. After weeks of running and hiding, of looking around every corner, of sleepless nights wondering if we'd be found, we were finally free.

We returned to find Gail going about her business as if nothing dramatic had ever taken place. I was sick with worry when Preston told me that she'd been tied to a chair and gagged, but she'd handled it like a real pro.

"I'm so sorry about everything," I said after Preston and I rushed in to supposedly save her.

She laughed. "Oh, honey. I enjoyed the excitement. Granted that I was a little worried there when those clowns tied me up, but it was clear that they were amateurs who didn't really know what the hell they were doing. That girl had tied me up so loosely, I didn't even need the knife that she left me to get myself free. The minute they were gone, I simply pulled my hands free. It was child's play."

"I'm happy to hear it," I said. "When Preston told me the state he'd left you in, I was beside myself with fear for your safety."

"Thank you for all you've done for us," Preston said.

"And thank you for all you've done for me," Gail said. "But you kids look a mess."

"We were hoping to clean up and…"

"You know your way around," Gail said, gesturing toward the guesthouse that had been our home for the last blissful days.

We headed out, took a quick shower, got into some clean clothes and headed back to say our final goodbyes to Gail.

"You kids have fun now that all the drama is over."

"We will," I said. "Thank you once again for everything. You went above and beyond…"

"It was fun having you, Priscilla," she said. "Anytime. Anytime you want to come back… you're more than welcomed."

We headed back into the city, our muscles finally letting go. Our breathing finally back to normal. The stress finally gone.

As Preston pulled up in front of the hotel we'd originally been staying at, he hesitated.

"How about a fresh start?" he said. "New day, new hotel, new start."

"I'm with you," I said.

And it was indeed a fresh start. We went to one of the most exclusive hotels in the city and booked a luxury suite that took up the entire corner of the hotel, giving us views of the mountains and a major part of the city.

Prick*ly Promise (Prickly Proposal #2)

The large room had an impressive sitting area and a closed off bedroom complete with its own luxury bathroom that included a therapeutic bath.

"This is even better than the room we originally had," I said, looking out the window, looking over the city that I loved so much.

But the hairs at the back of my neck stood on end... why?

Preston and me. Who were we? What were we?

The dynamic between us had changed and I was no longer sure where we stood. His invitation to spend the weekend in Vegas had surprised me, but... was this just a goodbye tryst?

Turning away from the window I looked at him, busily checking out the channels on the large screen television.

What now?

The question was on my lips, fighting to get out, but I held them in.

Was I afraid of the answer?

Without a doubt, yes. I didn't want to know that it was over. I wanted it all to continue, whether it was a charade or not, I wanted to go on... with him.

"Hey," he said, fully enthused. "That guy who won that talent show... you know... the magician. He's in town. How about we catch his show?"

While I wasn't a big fan of magicians, I smiled. "Sure."

He looked at me and flicked the television off. "Why don't you get settled in and I'm going to head out for a while?"

My heart sank. *Shit! Really? Head out for a while?*

He grabbed one of the cardkeys and headed to the door and my mind screamed a deluge of questions.

Where are you going?
How long will you be gone?
What will you be doing?

258

Shit. Shit! Shit!!

In stunned silence, I watched him leave.

For a solid five minutes I just stood there, going over in my mind the events of the past days, the past hours, the past minutes.

Shit. He was so sweet... almost loving.

Right?

Then... what the fuck!?

I finally shook off my indignation and opened my little travel bag. I'd packed quickly when we'd left San Angelo. I still had only my tiny little silver dress that was adequate for a night on the town. I pulled it out of the bag and shook it off.

It looked awful. Wrinkled and crinkled and looking as if... well, as if it'd spent the last few days stuffed into a bag.

Bringing it to the sink in the bathroom, I rinsed it out and hung it up to dry, hoping that it would remedy the situation. But looking at it, I knew it was hopeless.

I need a new dress, I thought.

Okay. Fine. If Preston can leave me to go out on the town, why can't I?

Good.

I grabbed my purse and with a determined step, headed to the door. My heart pounded as I opened the door, hoping beyond hope that Preston would be there.

But he wasn't.

Grow up. The fantasy is over.

I walked down the corridor to the elevator and pressed the button. The doors parted.

I gasped. My breath caught in my throat and my heart flipped out.

There he was, more gorgeous than ever.

Please don't ever leave me again, I wanted to say.

Too desperate?

I didn't care.

He held a few shopping bags in his hands.

My heart leapt with joy.

Silly girl.

I don't care. I'm happy to see him.
Silly, silly girl.

"Thought we could use some fresh clothes," he said with a smile that said just how pleased with himself he was.

"Good idea," I said, all while wanting to ask why he hadn't simply told me of his plans.

"I wanted to surprise you," he said, reading my mind.

"It worked. I'm surprised."

"Were you going somewhere?" he said as he stepped out of the elevator.

"Um." I struggled to find an explanation as to why I was standing in front of the elevator. "Ice," I finally said. "I thought I would get us some ice."

"No need," he said, leading me back to our room. "We're heading out, remember?"

The moment we entered the room, he held his shopping bag up to me. "Hope you'll like it."

I'm sure I will.

"This one's for you," he said as he pulled out a silky black backless minidress.

I practically ripped it out of his hand, excited by the idea of something fresh, new and not made of denim. "I'll go try it on."

I slipped into the bedroom and return seconds later with the fabulous and sexy dress that fit perfectly.

"Wow," Preston said as I walked out. "And to think that the girl at the shop said that very few women could make that dress work. I would just love to parade you down there and show her just how well you make that work."

I was thrilled by his flattering words.

"My turn," he said as he disappeared into the bedroom for a few moments.

He returned wearing black slacks, a silver-gray shirt and new shoes.

"I'm ready to hit the town," he said. "How about you?"

"Lead the way."

With no particular goal in mind, we strolled down the Strip until we found a restaurant we liked. After a sumptuous meal, we headed out to see a show, but not the magician Preston had hoped to see.

While he was disappointed, he nonetheless enjoyed the singer that we ended up seeing.

We finished the night off with a bit of gambling at a nearby casino, then finally headed back to our hotel room.

"I'm exhausted," I said as I plopped back onto the bed.

Preston stood in front of me. With his hot gaze on warming my body, he unbuttoned his shirt and slowly peeled it back, revealing his hard-working muscles.

"That's a shame," he said as he began to work his way out of his pants. "I was just getting started."

I sat up and kicked off my sandals. "I'm exhausted… in a good way. Like from so much fun, from such an exciting evening, but ready for more."

With a simple flick of his fingers, he unfastened the straps of my dress, letting it fall and pool around my hips.

"Tonight," he said, "with no other distractions, with no charades, with no worries… it's just you and me."

He leaned in to kiss me, laying me back onto the bed and slowly and gently making love to me. But while he was tender and loving, the words that I longed to hear didn't come.

Again and again, he made love to me, his kisses hungry, his caresses sensual and heated, and his murmurings hushed.

Still, the words never came.

With him breathing into my ear, I fell asleep, secure in his arms, but still so unsure of what the future held for us.

The next morning, we had breakfast in bed and got dressed for the day.

"You know that magician who won that contest that I wanted to see last night? Bobby

Crossland?" Preston said as we set out to tour the town. "He's playing at a casino nearby and this time I wrangled us two great tickets for the show tonight."

"But I thought you wanted to go back to your ranch as soon as possible."

"It can wait another day."

I smiled, happy to be staying in Vegas one more day.

That night, we arrived at the venue, and I was surprised to see that Preston had managed to get tickets in the front row.

"I don't know about this," I said. "You know how these things go. They always hassle the people seated up front."

"Come on," he said as he sat down and patted the seat beside him. "It'll be fun."

The venue filled up, the lights went down and then a spotlight opened onto a lone man in the middle of the stage.

"Good evening, tourists, travelers and magic enthusiasts. Have we got a show for you tonight." Instantly, he warmed the crowd.

Bobby Crossland was amusing, making jokes as he pretended to fumble through his magic tricks.

Midway through his act, he came to the edge of the stage and looked out into the audience.

"Ha, ha," he said with a clap of his hands. "This is the part of the show that many of you dread, isn't it? The part where I need an assistant." He scanned the crowd. "Oh. So many people looking down at their feet all of a sudden."

The crowd seated at a safe distance chuckled while many up front held their breaths.

"Let's see," Bobby said. "Who will it be?"

He looked straight at me.

Hell no.

"What's your name, miss?" he said.

Oh, hell no.

Preston nudged me with his elbow.

"Priscilla," I said.

266

"Oh!" he said with a laugh. "What an interesting name."

I fully expected an Elvis joke, but none came.

"I think that you would be perfect for this next trick."

I shook my head.

"Don't be shy," he said. "I promise that I won't saw you in half." He looked out at the audience. "That is so passé."

"Go on," Preston said, nudging me again with his elbow.

Grumbling my protest, I reluctantly got out of my seat, took the steps at the side of the stage and made my way up. If the man knew just how I dreaded going to him, he wouldn't have smiled so broadly.

"Now, I couldn't help but notice what a beautiful bracelet you have there." He pointed to my wrist.

I raised my wrist up to show the delicate silver chain with the small heart locket on it.

"Would you mind?" Not waiting for an answer, Bobby removed my bracelet and place it in a small, black velvet pouch.

Frowning, I glanced at Preston who was annoyingly amused by the situation.

"Now, this bracelet... is this just a trinket or a family heirloom?" Bobby said.

I shrugged. "Just a trinket."

"Good," he said. "So you won't mind if I take this trinket and turn it into..." With dramatic flair, he crumpled up the velvet bag, then opened it to retrieve a kitchen sponge.

The crowd booed.

"Hold on. Hold on," he said, holding up a silencing hand to the audience. He looked at me. "Do you want your bracelet back, or would you prefer the sponge?"

"My bracelet, please."

"But it is a pretty nice sponge."

I shook my head.

"Have it your way." He put the sponge back into the bag, scrunched it up then pulled out a ping pong ball. Again the crowd booed and again, I told him that I wanted my bracelet back.

Once again, he placed the ball in the bag, crumpled it up and pulled out a wedding veil.

"Oh, now that's funny," he said. "Any plans to get married by any chance? After all, this is Las Vegas; city of a million weddings."

I let out a nervous laugh. "No."

"You sure?"

I shook my head and he put the veil back in the bag and pulled out a bouquet of white flowers... a bridal bouquet.

"Are you sure you're not getting married?"

I shook my head.

He looked out into the audience and found Preston. "I think the universe is sending you a message, man."

Preston shrugged uncomfortably, obviously unhappy about being put on the spot.

Growing increasingly uncomfortable myself, I held back from simply stomping off the stage, bracelet or not.

"Okay," Bobby said. "Last chance. Let's see if we can't get the little lady's bracelet back."

He crumpled up the bag and pulled out a beautiful diamond ring. I stared at the ring, dumbfounded.

The audience let out a hush coo and then I felt a presence at my side. I looked up to see Preston standing there beside me.

The audience grew louder.

"Priscilla Pinkerton," Preston said as he took the ring from Bobby and got down on one knee. "I love you and want to spend my life with you."

The audience went wild, clapping, yelling and whistling.

"Will you marry me?" Preston said.

"I will!" a woman from the audience shouted out.

I looked into Preston's eyes, so filled with love, so filled with desire.

"Yes," I whispered.

"What was that?" Bobby said, bringing his microphone closer to me.

"Yes," I said. "Yes!"

As Preston pulled me into his arms, everyone in the audience got to their feet and applauded as if they were personally invested in our relationship.

I floated on a cloud as we returned to our seats and the remainder of the show was a blur.

With the show finally over, we headed out into the night air. After only a few steps, Preston turned to me.

"So," he said. "Do you really?"

"Huh?"

"I realize the pressure that you were under… you know… a proposal in front of everyone. Perhaps you just didn't want to let me down in front of a large crowd. So, I ask you. Do you really want to marry me?"

"Yes!" I shouted. "Of course, yes! How could you doubt it?"

He pulled me into his arms and kissed me.

As we walked on, heading back to our hotel, the gears in my head turned as I started planning for the wedding.

"While we're here in Vegas, why not have a small ceremony in a cute little chapel?" I said. "There's one on..."

Preston stopped walking and shook his head.

"But all we have to do is get the wedding license and find the chapel that we like and..."

He continued to shake his head. "Let me take care of this."

"What? An Elvis wedding?"

Gripping my shoulders, he looked into my eyes. "This is going to be a Prickly/Packard wedding. Just let me take care of everything."

"But..."

"Just relax and leave it to me."

"But I..."

He pressed his index finger to his lips and winked.

"Leave it to me," he whispered.

Chapter 20

<u>Priscilla</u>

After another day of enjoying the city sights, we boarded Preston's plane and headed back to San Angelo.

"You could at least give me a little clue as to what you have in mind," I said as I looked down on the Grand Canyon below.

"But that would spoil the surprise," he said with a chuckle. "In the meantime, I need to check in and see how things are going at the ranch. I've left Bacon and Rick alone for far too long.

As we had left the hotel and headed to the airport, a part of me was sad to leave Vegas. I had hoped to stay a little longer, and with Preston's proposal, I couldn't imagine not taking advantage of all the wedding options that were available to us.

But as we neared San Angelo, my heart pounded with excitement. A sense of coming home filled me... surprised me.

As we landed, Bacon and Rick came out to greet us.

"Hey, guys," Preston said as he hopped off the plane.

"Back so soon, boss?" Bacon said with a grin.

Then they saw me come out of the plane.

"Oh," Rick let out. "And you're not alone."

"Why am I not surprised," Bacon said. "Look at you two. You're meant for one another."

"I've got a lot of work to do," Preston said with a laugh. "So, let's get at it."

As we settled back into ranch living, Preston was constantly on the phone or back in town to make some sort of arrangement or other.

Finally, only a week after our return to Texas, he came to me.

"This is the day," he said.

"Today?" I said, startled. "But I… I'm not ready."

"You're not ready to marry me?"

"Yes. No. I mean. I'm ready to marry you, but…" Holding my hands out to expose myself, I looked down at my dusty jeans and faded blue t-shirt. "I'm not ready."

He smiled. "Calm down. Head into the shower, then put this on." He reached into his closet and pulled out a simple but gorgeous white dress. "No fuss. No muss. This is my idea of a big wedding."

He winked as he left me. "I'll be back in a few minutes with your first surprise."

I took a long hot shower, braided my hair in one long braid that I brought to the front, then got into the dress that fit so perfectly. Just as I finished putting on a pair of turquoise earrings, I heard a knock at the door.

Frowning, I wondered why Preston would knock. Playing along, I got up and opened the door.

"Dad?" I whispered, shocked by the sight of my father. "Dad!?"

"Priscilla," he said, tears in his eyes.

I ran into his arms then noticed Preston standing behind him.

"How? Why? Oh, Preston. How did you do this?" With my arm still around my father's waist, I looked at my husband-to-be.

"It's complicated," Preston said. "Suffice it to say that my father pulled a few strings. New evidence was suddenly brought forth and... well, here we are."

I had so many questions, so many things that I wanted to know. But for now, the important thing was that my father was there on my big day.

"I thought it was important that he be here to walk you down the aisle and give the bride away."

I smiled at Preston. "Thank you."

"And now," Preston said. "I'll give you two a moment and I'll be waiting for you downstairs."

"There's so much that I want to say, Dad," I said. "We have too much to say to one another."

He nodded. "In due time, my girl. Now is not the time to get into all that. This is your big day, and I'm thrilled to take part in it. Give me the honor of giving you away to a man who clearly loves you beyond all."

I smiled and nodded. Setting my hand on his forearm, I let him lead me down the stairs and out the back patio door to where chairs had been set up and guests awaited my arrival.

Immediately I spotted Gail who already had tears of joy streaming down her cheeks. Then to my surprise, I noticed that Tip was there. For a moment, my heart skipped a beat, wondering how he was there, but then I noticed Rick chatting with him.

Then I saw Preston standing at the altar, gorgeous, proud and looking at me with an intensity that thrilled me.

Our vows were simple and traditional. An old friend of Preston's sang a beautiful song and then...

It was time to party.

Preston had prepared a rodeo themed wedding, with cowboys, great country music and plenty of food and drink.

With a glass of beer in my hand, I walked over to Tip, eager to learn how it came to be that he was at my wedding.

"Congratulations, Priscilla," he said.

"It goes without saying. I'm surprised to see you."

He nodded. "Your husband is a very understanding and forgiving man. I was surprised and thrilled when he called. As for you, I do hope that you understand that..."

"I understand, Tip," I said, suddenly pleased that Preston had seen through Tip's empty threats and had invited him. "I wasn't too pleased by your tactic, but I understand."

"Good." His shoulders relaxed. "This is a nasty business sometimes. I hope you know that I would never have hurt…"

I put my hand to his shoulder. "I know, Tip. I even told Preston that I couldn't believe that you would ever hurt anyone or anything."

I smiled at him. He seemed suddenly so much older… tired and worn out.

"I began another case here in San Angelo," he said. "A bitch of a case." He wiped his brow. "This business is killing me."

"Oh?" I said, surprised.

"Yeah…" He looked up at me from under his sweaty brow. "This'll be my last hunt."

"The last one here in San Angelo?"

"No. The last one. Period. I'm hanging up my bounty hunting boots."

"Well, you certainly deserve to take it easy for a while." I patted his shoulder. "Enjoy the day, Tip. This should be fun."

I left him and meandered through the crowd of guests. In the distance, Gail was chatting with Bacon while near the large buffet table that had been set up, my father was in an intense conversation with Rick.

Spotting Preston as he watched kids who tried to ride his sheep, I walked up to him, and nuzzled my way under his arm.

"Is this to your liking?" he said, scanning the grounds that were filled with activity.

"It's perfect." I looked at him. "I'm happy that Gail came... and my father... Wow. What a surprise. I just spoke to Tip, and we talked it out. But..."

"But what?"

"Where's your father? Why didn't he come?"

Preston shrugged. "The treatment that he's on is pretty rough on him. While he is getting a bit better, he is still too weak to travel. Maybe sometime soon, we can go out there to see how he's doing."

"Sounds good." I wanted to ask about his father's involvement with my father's imprisonment. More specifically, what part had his father played in having my father freed? I wondered how much he knew. Preston had not yet said anything about the documents that he'd signed. Did the document included any kind of admission regarding my father's imprisonment?

In the end, I simply smiled at Preston and decided to enjoy the day. The many questions that I had would be answered someday.

"Hey, lovebirds," Gail shouted as she came up behind us. "This is by far the most original wedding I've ever attended."

"Are you ready to take a ride on a bull?" Preston said.

She burst out laughing. "Not quite. I just wanted to come and congratulate your two. You guys had me worried there for a while, but I'm happy to see that everything worked out."

"So am I," I said as I leaned into Preston.

"I have to say, Priscilla, as far as lifestyles go…" She looked around the immensity of the grounds, the bright blue sky and the sheep grazing in the distance. "This is pretty hard to beat."

I nodded. She was right. While it wasn't quite where I'd imagined my life would lead me, it was a pleasant surprise. I'd already forgotten all about my life back in Vegas and I looked forward to my life with my husband right there on the ranch.

"Do you plan on giving up your bounty hunting days?" Gail said.

I looked at Preston then glanced at Tip who was talking with my father. "I don't know," I finally said. "I was thinking of taking over Tip's business… my boss… and then… well, I'll see what I can do here in Texas under the Pinkerton umbrella.

Working with my dad would be fun and a great way to reconnect."

Preston looked at me, surprised but pleased. "Looks like you've got it all figured out."

Epilogue

Preston

Priscilla's plan to take over Tip's business didn't quite work out as she'd planned. Only one month after the wedding, she came to me, distraught and worried.

"What's the matter?" I said, rushing to her side.

She was flushed and breathless as she came into the house and fell back into the sofa.

"Priscilla," I said. "What's going on?"

"I just came back from the doctor," she said.

I took a step back, not certain I wanted to hear it. With my father struggling to get better, I couldn't bear the thought of something happening to my new bride.

"I think you should sit down, Preston," she said, patting the cushion beside her on the sofa.

I sat down, my heart pounding. I reached out to take her hands in mine.

"I think that we might be in for a big change in our lives. I know that this is unexpected, and I don't know how you'll take the news… what with your father sick and all, but…"

"Oh, heavens, Priscilla. You're killing me. What's wrong?"

"From now on, it won't just be the two of us."

Frowning, I looked at her. "What… is your father coming to live with us?"

"No," she said as she smiled and placed her hands lovingly over her belly.

"A baby?" I squealed. "You're pregnant?"

She nodded, her cheeks red with excitement. "Are you happy?"

"Am I happy? Of course, I'm happy."

"Will you be doubly happy if there are two?"

I pulled her into my arms and held her tight, thanking the heavens for bringing her into my life. "I'm thrilled. More than thrilled. I want a houseful of kids and starting off with two just gives us a head start."

She leaned back into the cushions, relieved and blissful.

"You know," she said after a moment. "All of this is because of your father."

I shot her a quizzical glance. "Huh?"

"If your father hadn't hired me to find you... if we hadn't been thrown off track by some rather odd behavior on his part... if we hadn't been so scared of him and run off to hide... we wouldn't be here today... together... and expecting twins."

"Well, then I guess I owe my dear old dad a load of gratitude."

"Two," she said quietly, holding up two fingers. "Two babies."

"We have plenty of room," I said.

"Yeah, but it would be nice to have a helping hand," she said. "I wish my mother could be here to help me. I wish she was here to share the news with me."

Unfortunately, Priscilla had learned that her mother had drank herself to death following the imprisonment of her husband. While distraught, she hadn't been too surprised by the news.

"I wish she could be here for you, too, but…" I looked at her. I hadn't yet told her the news that I'd just recently received. "Perhaps my mother could come and help out."

She guffawed. "Very funny, Preston. Your mother passed away, remember?"

I shook my head. "No, she didn't."

"What do you mean, no? Preston. You told me over and over again that you suspected your father of killing your mother."

"And I was wrong."

"So? Where is she? Why didn't she come to the wedding?"

"You know those papers I signed for my father?"

She nodded. "Yeah. The papers that you haven't told me anything about yet."

"One of those documents gave me the right to know about my mother's medical records."

"Oh?"

"Penelope Prickly... formerly Packard... had a nervous breakdown... or something like that. She's been institutionalized for these past years."

"Oh, Preston. I'm so sorry."

"Turns out that my father had nothing to do with her disappearance... well, at least not in the manner that I suspected. She had been showing signs of being unstable. But my father finally had her committed when he found her out for a walk completely nude... in the middle of winter. It was one of the coldest winters we'd ever had, and she'd gone out, barefoot and without a stitch of clothing. When he brought her inside, she insisted that I was out there lost, but I was really in my room sleeping.

He'd had a terrible time convincing her to stay inside and get warm."

Priscilla gasped and reached out for my hand.

"After that, he didn't trust her to be alone."

"So, he, in essence, saved her life."

I nodded. "He also realized that she was in no condition to tend to Penelope Trust… so he had it put in my name but managed everything. I've looked at the books… he ran it very well… very profitable."

"And you're going to take over that now?"

"Yeah. That's the other part of what I signed. Penelope Trust is mine… as is the Packard fortune that my mother inherited."

She sat quiet and pensive for a moment. "But, Preston, if your mother is mentally ill or unstable, she won't be of any use to me here."

I shook my head. "For years they didn't know what was wrong with her… or what to do about it. But the letter that I received a few days ago is very optimistic. Her doctors say that she's been responding well to a new medication."

Clapping her hands against her lap, Priscilla stood and looked down on me. "Wait a minute. All this time? All this time you've thought that your mother was dead when in truth she's..."

I nodded. "... been recuperating from a severe trauma."

"Does she want to be in your life? Is she troubled by her past?"

"I received a letter from her this morning. She's fully aware of her troubled past. She knows who I am, and she misses me. She was devastated when I told her that I had just been married. She would have liked to attend the wedding. She would have like to meet my bride... my wife. But now, Priscilla..." I reached out to take her hand and stood to face her. "When I tell her of our children to come... of her grandchildren... She'll be the happiest woman alive."

"Then let's invite her over for dinner. I'll invite my father and we can have your father with us via the internet. The whole family... together to celebrate the future to come... bigger, better, united."

How could I have ever doubted how much I loved her? Beyond her physical beauty, Priscilla had a heart of gold, a heart that I knew my mother would appreciate and a heart that would give our children all the love they needed.

"You're crying," Priscilla said.

"I never thought that I could be this happy... and it's all because of you. If bounty hunting is what brought us together... you should never give it up."

And that's the end for now! Thank you for reading the Prickly Proposal Series.

Hi Guys, I want to ask for a favor. If you enjoyed the Prickly Proposal Series and want more books like this from me, I would greatly appreciate your review here:

https://www.amazon.com/gp/product/B09VKJ5 1MN

And

I love hearing from you and would like to keep in touch with you!

JOIN THE FAM!

Rachel Angel Newsletter
http://madmimi.com/signups/5e9ebf668aa14b4890d8 affb0ce952f9/join

Prick*ly Promise (Prickly Proposal #2)

Rachel Angel Reader Group called Rachel Angel
Royal Readers
https://www.facebook.com/groups/881277658892159/

Rachel Angel Facebook Page
https://www.facebook.com/RachelAngelBooks/

Rachel Angel Bookbub
https://www.bookbub.com/authors/rachel-angel

Rachel's Amazon Author Page
https://www.amazon.com/Rachel-Angel/e/B00EHA11DO

Rachel Angel Goodreads Page
https://www.goodreads.com/author/show/7211708.Rachel
_Angel

Rachel Angel Twitter
https://twitter.com/RachelRomances

Rachel Angel Instagram
https://www.instagram.com/rachelangelbooks/

About the Author

RACHEL ANGEL
Bio

An USA Today bestselling author, Rachel Angel writes stories about Strong Feisty Women and the men they tame in RH, Bully Romances, Dark Romances, Fantasy, PNR, and sexy billionaire Romances. Rachel Angel is a pen name for a million-selling author who worked as an executive at Fortune 50 corporations, in legal and production at cable television channels and at the Walt Disney Corporation. Besides being a full time author with various pen names, she appears in front of the camera as a television host, voiceover artist, and is a frequent guest on top 15 National Radio as an authority on women's issues, the entertainment industry, and women empowerment. Her non-fiction books have been number one bestsellers, used by organizations such as the US Mental Health Association. Pushing the edge of romance, books published under Rachel Angel explores the hidden, dark, and even deepest desires of human romances, while featuring strong female leads.

MORE BOOK SERIES FROM RACHEL ANGEL

BAD BOY ROYALS OF KINGSBURY PREP (Complete)
RH New Adult/High School Bully Dark Contemporary Romance – HEAT 4 out of 5

Tempest and The Black Envelope (Books 1 and 2) with Bonus and Clue on the Treasure
https://www.amazon.com/dp/B07Z44T1PF

Revenge
https://www.amazon.com/gp/product/B07SQP3HL3

Secret Princess
https://www.amazon.com/dp/B07YLHJ38K

Fallen Royals
https://www.amazon.com/dp/B07XXC625K

Prick*ly Promise (Prickly Proposal #2)

Reign of Rebels
https://www.amazon.com/dp/B07XM3FKW6

Complete Series Box Set
https://www.amazon.com/gp/product/B08781CS94

Kingmakers of Kingsbury Series
RH Bully Fantasy Paranormal Shifter Fae
Romance – HEAT 4 out of 5

Long before there was an All-Royals Academy called Kingsbury Prep, there was the Kingmaker and her kings.

As Violet Kingsbury, I was born to be a kingmaker. In a time when wars were common and thrones were fought after, the only name that could bring about peace...the only man that could trump the decrees of kings was Kingsbury. The Kingmaker. But when the legendary Kingmaker is disposed, and the time of the Choosing has come, can I, the daughter of The Kingmaker rise to take the place of my father? I am about to find out as the strongest, most capable, and most

Prick*ly Promise (Prickly Proposal #2)

legendary princes across the lands come to challenge me for the Choosing including 4 of the most handsome princes who not only wants to win, but to want to win me, too:
Avery
Axel
Reggie
Ollie

*Becoming Kingmaker, even as The Kingmaker's daughter, will not be easy in a male world where ladies were supposed to be damsels who needed saving. To become Kingmaker, I will prove to all, especially the princes, that I am here to stay, and will be the one doing the saving. **Kingmakers of Kingsbury Series, is a Reverse Harem Bully Romance with mixed genres elements, action, and mature scenes recommended for age 17 and up.*

Kingmaker's Kings (Book 1)
https://www.amazon.com/dp/B082QMNCW4
Kingmaker's Kiss (Book 2) (May 18, 2020)
https://www.amazon.com/gp/product/B084BZYW28

Kingmaker's Kill (Book 3) (July 28, 2020)
https://www.amazon.com/gp/product/B084BT8154

Prick*ly Promise (Prickly Proposal #2)

HEARTBREAK FALLS

RH Bully Dark New Adult/High School Romance Mystery – HEAT 4 out of 5

With a name like Heartbreak Falls, one didn't expect to find love at the new town I had moved to courtesy of my new stepfamily aka Mom's new husband and his sons.

Something was up with my new rich stepfather, his sons, and what happened to their last stepmother. Something was up with the entire town, which my stepfamily seem to run. Along with the school where my stepbrothers reigned as cruel princes. All 3 of them were known as The Heartbreakers. Two were twins and my age, and then there was Tristan, the oldest. Gorgeous but god-awful hateful to me. What was up? I was about to find out...if I lived long enough.
**Heartbreak Falls is a RH Dark Bully Romance and mystery for 18 and up. It is YA/NA and has themes of bullying and sex. If that's fine with you, then dig in! Bully Me Not is book 1 of 5 and contains a cliffhanger.
Bully Me Not

Prick*ly Promise (Prickly Proposal #2)

Bully Me Not
https://www.amazon.com/dp/B07XNQV36Q

Break Me Not
https://www.amazon.com/dp/B07XX7HZZZ

Dare Me Not
https://www.amazon.com/dp/B07Z4369V7

Destroy Me Not
https://www.amazon.com/gp/product/B084C143VR

Love Me Not
https://www.amazon.com/gp/product/B084BTRVYN

HOUSE

RH Dark College New Adult Romance – HEAT 5 out of 5

It was his last will and testament.

For one week, four of us was to live together. Play nice to each other like we used to when we were kids.

Seb, Thomas, Ashford and me.

Three of Mr. Keystone's sons and me, the maid's daughter.

All those years, the three sons bullied and ridiculed me because I was the maid's daughter.

So, why was I back? Why did I cared to be in the same house as those three tormentors?

Because I was in Mr. Keystone's will.

He had always been kind to me, even if his sons weren't, so I could only honor his wishes. And he was like a father to me, and didn't treat me like the maid's daughter. But as soon as I could, I left to go to college. Two years ago. Meanwhile, the boys went their separate ways, too. Estranged from each other.

So why was I here having to live in the same house with his sons for a week?

I don't know, but I'm about to find out, even if it meant my old adolescent feelings for all three of them might surface again. And if being in the mansion we called a house together might jog some memories of the wild nights we've had here.

It's just one week. I could survive that. Or could I?

***House is the first book in The House Series, which is a Reverse Harem Dark College Romance recommended for age 18+ due to mature themes.*

House (The House Series, Book #1)
https://www.amazon.com/gp/product/B0863Z36S5

Haven (The House Series, Book #2)
https://www.amazon.com/gp/product/B087BFJWK5
Habit (The House Series, Book #3)
https://www.amazon.com/gp/product/B087B6MZDM
HEIRS (The House Series, Book #4)
https://www.amazon.com/gp/product/B087BCKS27
Haunt (The House Series, Book #5)

Prick*ly Promise (Prickly Proposal #2)

https://www.amazon.com/gp/product/B087BGL27P
Home (The House Series, Book #6)
https://www.amazon.com/gp/product/B08966PF77

FALLEN FAE ACADEMY

RH Bully Romance Fantasy Paranormal Fae – HEAT 4 out of 5

"At Fallen Fae Academy, the magic will either complete you or kill you."

My name is Harley, as in Harlequin. Plucked from my home from Las Vegas, NV, and placed into an University on an arts scholarship, suddenly I am the girl the four hottest and most popular boys have decided to "initiate".

This is no ordinary "hazing" ritual, and these boys are no ordinary boys.

This mysterious University looks like any ivy league campus, but it isn't. Step in and you are transported beyond your wildest imagination. I should be ecstatic being here. Except surviving "Initiation" is going to take everything I've got.

Prick*ly Promise (Prickly Proposal #2)

Don't let the beauty of the four fae boys fool you. They are as dangerous as they are beautiful. And underneath everything, runs a deep secret. One I need to find out before Initiation kills me.

They think a human is weak. They think I shouldn't be at this university. I'm about to prove them wrong.

**The Fallen Fae Series is a 6-book RH Academy College Bully Romance Series featuring a badass heroine, four deadly, striking fae princes, heart-pounding action, super steamy love scenes, and great romance.

Initiation: Year 1 Fallen Fae Academy Book 1
https://www.amazon.com/Initiation-Year-Academy-Reversed-Paranormal-ebook/dp/B07V9L8LHD

Transformation: Year 2 Fallen Fae Academy Book 2
https://www.amazon.com/dp/B07WWFXVCH

Declaration: Year 3 Fallen Fae Academy Book 3
https://www.amazon.com/gp/product/B07XLMS.GDJ

Interruption War Year 3 (Fallen Fae Academy #4)

Prick*ly Promise (Prickly Proposal #2)

https://www.amazon.com/dp/B0833JC8YJ

Disruption (Fallen Fae Academy #5)
https://www.amazon.com/dp/B084DB7F1B

Succession (Fallen Fae Academy Book #6)
https://www.amazon.com/dp/B084D4VRCY

Fallen Fae Academy Box Set Part 1 (Books 1 -3)
https://www.amazon.com/gp/product/B08772LQFT

FALLEN FAE B. I. Series

RH Paranormal Romance Fantasy – HEAT 4 out of 5

Fae-ther Issues (Fallen Fae B.I. Book #1) Coming in 2021!

Now that it is changeling Harley's Mission to find and capture the rogue dark fae her evil father has unleashed into the human world, Harley leaves the opulence of her mother's kingdom in the Faery

Realms. to return to her human adopted parents' home in Las Vegas to start her career as a trainee FBI agent. Piece of cake, isn't it, especially since she has finally discovered and mastered the powerful fae magic she went through the Fallen Fae Academy to learn. When a series of unusual murders show up along the Strip, and a close friend becomes the suspect, Harley would never have guess who would show up to give her some advice and clue to solve the murders…her evil dark fae wizard father. But could she trust him? Meanwhile the four princes from her Fallen Fae Academy days grapple with her decision to live in Las Vegas instead of assuming the throne of her kingdom in the Faery Realms.

https://www.amazon.com/dp/B08L63B29D

Fae-mous (Fallen Fae B.I. Book #2)

Harley's last case took her from casino to casino along the Las Vegas Strip in search of a killer who may have been a rogue dark fae, who wield a power she had yet to encounter. With the aid of her former classmates and still current lovers from Fallen Fae Academy, Harley devise a scheme to lure out the killer. Things become complicated when Harley and her guys discover the unusual murders before were a mere distraction from a bigger plot, her father and the rogue dark fae minions he had unleashed, had planned and had already set into motion…one that involves Las Vegas' former past as an Atomic bomb testing site to the beginning of the Apocalypse.

https://www.amazon.com/Fae-mous-Adult-Paranormal-Romance-Fallen-ebook/dp/B08LCDCTDK

Fae-ful (Fallen Fae B.I. Book #3)

The clock is ticking. Harley and her guys must figure out the clues where the rogue dark fae army will unleash their dark magic and destroy the human race. Using the powers of all the kingdoms. In the faery realms, Harley and her four fae princes' powers converge to fight the power of the dark fae in the fight of their lifetimes.

<u>CRUEL PRINCES OF WYVERN ALL-BOYS ACADEMY</u>

(RH Bully Romance Fantasy Paranormal Shifters) - HEAT 4 out of 5

Enter the Wyvern All-Boys Academy as the Only Girl or Get Killed for Defying the Royal Decree

Diamonds and Dragons (Cruel Princes of Wyvern All-Boys Academy Book 1)
https://www.amazon.com/Diamonds-Dragons-Reverse-Fantasy-All-Boys-ebook/dp/B07SFV1PRH/

Roses and Emeralds (Cruel Princes of Wyvern All-Boys Academy Book 2)
https://www.amazon.com/Roses-Emeralds-Reverse-Fantasy-All-Boys-ebook/dp/B07TS1BKLT/

Silver and Starlight (Cruel Princes of Wyvern All-Boys Academy Book 3)

Prick*ly Promise (Prickly Proposal #2)

https://www.amazon.com/dp/B07VXVK2KV

Cruel Princes of Wyvern All-Boys Academy
Complete Series Box Set
https://www.amazon.com/gp/product/B086V6ZJKH

BAD BOYS BILLIONAIRE BACHELORS
CLUB (Standalone Novels)
Billionaire Romances – Heat 3 out of 5

Bidding on the Billionaire
https://www.amazon.com/gp/product/B07CB8VXFY

Movie Merger
https://www.amazon.com/gp/product/B07BX7DZ4G

Buying the Billionaire
https://www.amazon.com/gp/product/B07BXC37RQ

Broken
https://www.amazon.com/gp/product/B07BX97343

Prick*ly Promise (Prickly Proposal #2)